By the time the lovers were reunited in a classic Hollywood happy ending, Patty had made up her mind. She would make things up with Jim, no matter what it took. She loved him too much to let him go without a fight.

The lights came up in the movie theater, and Patty sniffled discreetly and felt in her purse for a tissue. "I'm a total cornball when it comes to romantic movies," she said, wiping away her tears.

Then she froze, not quite sure whether to believe her tear-misted eyes. Was she seeing things? Had the movie gotten to her that badly?

At the front of the movie theater, turning to head up the aisle in her direction, was Jim. And he wasn't alone. At his side was a beautiful black girl in a short purple dress, a wide purple headband in her dark curly hair. The girl was laughing. Then she said something to Jim, her face very close to his.

Patty couldn't believe it! The whole time she had been crying over him and wanting to get back together, he had been right in the same movie theater, cuddling up with another girl!

D0032720

Bantam Books in the Sweet Valley High Series
Ask your bookseller for the books you have missed

SWEET VALLEY HIGH

BOY TROUBLE

Written by
Kate William

Created by
FRANCINE PASCAL

BANTAM BOOK
NEW YORK · TORONTO · LONDON · SYDNEY · AUCKLAND

RL 6, IL age 12 and up

BOY TROUBLE
A Bantam Book / January 1990

Sweet Valley High is a registered trademark of Francine Pascal

Conceived by Francine Pascal

*Produced by Daniel Weiss Associates, Inc.,
33 West 17th Street,
New York, NY 10011*

Cover art by James Mathewuse

ISBN 0-553-28317-0

Published simultaneously in the United States and Canada

Bantam Books are published by Bantam Books, a division of Bantam Doubleday
Dell Publishing Group, Inc. Its trademark, consisting of the words "Bantam
Books" and the portrayal of a rooster, is Registered in U.S. Patent and Trademark
Office and in other countries. Marca Registrada, Bantam Books, 666 Fifth Avenue,
New York, New York 10103.

PRINTED IN THE UNITED STATES OF AMERICA

OPM   0 9 8 7 6 5 4 3

BOY TROUBLE

One

"So, Liz, when do you want to interview *me* for the new 'Personal Profiles' column?" Winston Egbert asked, flexing one of his thin arms in an exaggerated pose.

Elizabeth Wakefield laughed along with the rest of the group at the lunch table.

"The column is supposed to focus on people with real talent, not *ridiculous* talent," Todd Wilkins pointed out, grinning.

Winston pretended to be offended, and Elizabeth patted his hand. "You'll be the first Sweet Valley student I'll feature," she assured Winston, "*next* year. 'Personal Profiles' is about seniors. We've still got a year to go!"

"I'll let you off the hook this time, Wakefield." Winston wagged a finger at her. "But I won't let you forget that promise. I'd better not

1

catch you interviewing basketball hotshot Wilkins before me."

Elizabeth darted a smile at her boyfriend. Todd's brown eyes sparkled back at her. "Don't worry, Egbert," Todd said casually. "Sure, I have an in with the school paper, but I don't take advantage of it. I only make Liz put my picture in *The Oracle* every other week."

Elizabeth punched Todd's arm lightly. "Every third week," she jokingly corrected him. "Anyway, I'm glad you guys like the 'Personal Profiles' idea." She had hoped for a positive reaction from Winston, Enid Rollins, DeeDee Gordon, Bill Chase, and the other Sweet Valley juniors at the table.

"How are you going to have time to write two columns?" Bill asked.

"I've been wondering that myself," Elizabeth admitted. Interviewing people for "Personal Profiles" in addition to composing "Eyes and Ears," her weekly gossip column for *The Oracle*, would be a challenge. But she knew the more journalistic practice she got, the better writer she would be someday.

"It won't be hard if you mix business with pleasure," DeeDee suggested slyly. "Like by interviewing cute senior guys!"

Elizabeth laughed. "True. The first person I want to feature happens to be a girl, though—"

She broke off, her eyes lighting up with pleasure. "Hi, Jess!"

The others echoed the greeting as Jessica Wakefield stopped by their table to talk to her sister before heading off to sit with a group of her own friends. "Hi, yourself!" Jessica responded.

An outsider would have looked from Elizabeth to Jessica in a classic double take. Students at Sweet Valley High were used to the uncanny resemblance between the sixteen-year-old identical twins, however, and most people didn't have a hard time telling them apart. Elizabeth usually wore her silky, sun-streaked blond hair pulled back in barrettes or in a ponytail, while Jessica liked hers loose around her shoulders. Jessica's trendy clothes weren't for Elizabeth, who preferred neat khakis or the denim skirt she was wearing that day. Jessica liked bright colors, while Elizabeth usually wore soft pastels— although Jessica managed to find a number of Elizabeth's clothes satisfactory enough to borrow and then forget to return!

Elizabeth, older than Jessica by four minutes, had a gift for organization. There was a place in her life for everything that mattered to her— family, schoolwork, extracurricular activities, friends, and social life. But Jessica didn't bother to balance work and play. She was perfectly content to emphasize the latter. Jessica admired Elizabeth, even if she sometimes thought her twin acted too grown-up and serious. She was sure Elizabeth would become a famous writer, but as far as Jessica was concerned, the future was too far away to worry about now. Jessica was more interested in the present, in surrounding herself with her good friends Amy Sutton and Lila Fowler, and in being at the center of things in Sweet Valley, California. And anyone could see that she was an unqualified success at that.

Elizabeth turned to DeeDee. The petite junior was wearing a T-shirt with a bright abstract design. "I wanted to tell you, DeeDee, I love your shirt. Did you make it?"

"You really like it?" DeeDee asked, smiling shyly. "I'm wearing it as a sort of advertisement. There's a big crafts fair at the mall this weekend, and I'm going to exhibit my hand-painted T-shirts."

"Crafts fair," Jessica said. "You mean like handmade jewelry and stuff? Sounds like fun."

"I bet you'll be sold out in five minutes," Elizabeth predicted as Jessica drifted away to join another table.

DeeDee's boyfriend, the tall towheaded surfer Bill Chase, leaned forward. "She sure will, because I'll be there early to buy the whole batch," he said, putting an arm around DeeDee to give her a squeeze.

DeeDee rolled her eyes. "Yeah, right! I know

4

where *you'll* be on Saturday—catching a wave on your new surfboard!"

"Saturday . . . that reminds me." Elizabeth looked around the crowded school cafeteria. "Do you see Patty anywhere, DeeDee? I want to talk to her about being interviewed for 'Personal Profiles.' " Elizabeth thought Patty Gilbert, a talented dancer and a popular senior who also happened to be DeeDee's best friend, would get the new feature off to a great start.

"As a matter of fact, she's right over there." Elizabeth followed DeeDee's gaze and saw the pretty black girl setting her tray down a few tables away.

"But don't expect her to talk any sense to you," DeeDee warned, laughing. "You know her boyfriend, Jim Hollis? He's a freshman at Pacific College, and he's coming home this weekend for the first time in almost a month. Need I say more?"

Smiling, Elizabeth shook her head. She knew just how Patty must feel. Not long ago, Todd had been living in Vermont, three thousand miles from Sweet Valley! Elizabeth's heart had almost broken when his family moved to the East Coast. It had been impossible to maintain their old closeness—and for a time, she and Todd had gone their separate ways. But recently the Wilkinses had moved back to California, and now things were wonderful between

5

Elizabeth and Todd. Luckily for Patty, Pacific College was only two hours north of Sweet Valley.

"I think I'll go talk to her right now," Elizabeth decided. "I want to arrange an interview with her before the weekend gets here and we lose her for good!"

Patty Gilbert was sitting at a table with Olivia Davidson, the arts editor for *The Oracle*, Guy Chesney, and Emily Mayer, both of whom played in the popular Sweet Valley High band, The Droids.

"Don't tell me that's all you're eating, Patty," Olivia said.

Patty looked down at the small tossed salad on her tray. As a dancer, she was always conscious of her weight, although she didn't usually limit herself to rabbit food. "I'm dieting now because Jim's coming home for the weekend," she explained to Olivia. "I'm making a lot of special plans, most of which include food, like a picnic at the beach, a romantic dinner . . ."

Olivia laughed, and Patty joined in. She knew she was going overboard trying to come up with fun things to do. *The weekend just has to be perfect*, she thought for about the hundredth time since Jim had called from college to say he was driving down to Sweet Valley after his calculus exam on Friday.

In the past, she hadn't felt this sort of pressure. At first when Jim went to Pacific, he had come home every weekend, and they had talked on the phone several times a week. But lately he had been getting busier and busier—so busy that he had stayed on campus three weekends in a row. And he wasn't calling as often, either.

I wasn't going to worry about all that, Patty reminded herself. *Jim's got his own life, and I have mine*. But it had been hard lately not to feel a little anxious. One thing was for sure: They needed this weekend together if their romance was going to survive.

"Hey, you guys. Mind if I join you?"

Patty snapped out of her reverie and heard a chorus of hellos greeting Elizabeth Wakefield as she pulled a chair up to the table.

"Hi, Liz," Patty said. Although everyone liked Elizabeth, Patty felt she and Elizabeth shared a special bond since the time they had teamed up to help DeeDee regain her self-confidence by putting her in charge of the school talent show. "What's up?"

"Business for *The Oracle*, as usual," Elizabeth answered. "I'm launching a new feature for the newspaper, a series of interviews with seniors about their plans for the future and their mem-

7

orable experiences at Sweet Valley High. It's called 'Personal Profiles.' "

"Catchy title," Patty remarked.

"How would you like to be my first profile?" Liz inquired.

She smiled as Patty's dark, almond-shaped eyes widened in surprise. "Me?" Patty asked. "Are you kidding. I'd love to!"

Olivia nodded in approval. "Good choice," she said. "I like to see the arts well-represented."

"Great," Elizabeth said. "Tell you what, Patty. I'd like to get started as soon as possible. DeeDee said she didn't think you were doing much of anything this weekend—maybe we could get together on Saturday."

Patty's jaw dropped. "DeeDee said *what?*" Then she caught the mischievous twinkle in Elizabeth's eyes. "She told you about Jim, huh?" Patty guessed, grinning.

"Believe me, I know how you feel," Elizabeth assured her. "You must be dying to see him."

"I am," Patty admitted, running a hand through her long, black hair. "I miss him like crazy. Four weeks is too long to spend apart."

Elizabeth tilted her head. "I thought you two got together every weekend."

"Not recently. Jim's been too busy." The nagging doubt about their relationship returned, but Patty dismissed it with a decisive shake of

8

her head. She smiled brightly. "We'll really have to make up for lost time."

"Well, if you're not completely exhausted by Sunday night, do you want to meet for the interview then?" Elizabeth suggested.

"Sunday's fine with me," Patty agreed.

"Great. Can you come over to my house around seven?" Elizabeth asked. "We could talk over dessert."

"Perfect." Patty jotted a reminder to herself on the cover of her notebook as Elizabeth stood up to leave. "See you then, Liz!"

The bus dropped Patty off at the corner of Ocean Avenue and Ridgeview. It was just three blocks to her house, and Patty walked slowly, her duffle bag stuffed with workout clothes slung over one shoulder. She felt loose and relaxed after an invigorating class at the Modern Dance Academy downtown, the Southern California sun was shining—and in just two days Jim would be home!

Heading up the driveway, Patty hummed a tune from *West Side Story* to herself. *Mom's home early for once*, she observed, noting her mother's Buick in the garage. Patty guessed it had been a relatively slow day at the computer consulting firm where Mrs. Gilbert worked.

Inside, Patty headed for the kitchen and

immediately removed a pitcher of lemonade from the refrigerator. Her mother was on the telephone, talking animatedly. Glass in hand, Patty slid onto a stool.

Mrs. Gilbert cupped a hand over the mouthpiece. "It's Jana," she informed Patty.

"Give her my love!" Patty whispered.

"You can yourself pretty soon," Mrs. Gilbert quickly said. Then she resumed her conversation with Jana.

Patty raised her eyebrows at her mother's comment. *What's up with Jana?* she wondered. It had to be something good because Mrs. Gilbert was smiling from ear to ear.

Hearing from Patty's twenty-one-year-old sister, who had moved to San Francisco after her graduation from college, was always a big event. Between her job with a nonprofit environmental organization and her social life in the city, Jana had a busy schedule. She hadn't been home for a visit since she moved six months ago, and her phone calls were usually short and rushed.

Patty took a sip of her lemonade. "Get here as soon as you can, honey," Mrs. Gilbert was saying. "But promise you'll drive safely. I don't trust that old VW."

A moment later Mrs. Gilbert hung up the phone and turned to Patty. "Guess what? Jana's finally coming home, this weekend! Isn't that wonderful?"

This weekend? Patty's face fell.

Mrs. Gilbert caught her expression. "Honey, I thought you'd be thrilled."

"Oh, I am," Patty said. "I just have a bit of a conflict, that's all." *That's the understatement of the year!* she thought. "Jim's coming down from school, remember?"

"That's right." Mrs. Gilbert lifted her hands in a helpless gesture. "And Jana was dropping hints that she has some big news to tell all of us. She wants to have a real family weekend."

"Big news?" Patty was momentarily distracted. "And she didn't say what it was?"

Mrs. Gilbert shook her head. "No, she was very mysterious about it."

Patty sipped the last of her lemonade. "Maybe she got promoted at work," she guessed. "Or maybe she's moving back to Southern California!"

"I suppose we'll just have to wait and find out," Mrs. Gilbert said.

"Yeah," Patty agreed. Then her dilemma hit her full force. What was she going to do about Jim? She hadn't seen her sister in half a year. They had always been close, and Patty missed Jana's companionship. It would be fantastic to see Jana—there was so much for them to catch up on.

But Jim and I need this weekend, she reminded herself. *Our whole relationship might depend on it!*

She had to make a choice, unless she wanted to spend the entire weekend driving back and forth between her house and Jim's.

Mrs. Gilbert seemed to read her mind. "Is there any way you could ask Jim to visit another time?" she asked Patty as she rinsed a head of lettuce in the sink.

Patty sighed, her shoulders slumping. "I guess I should call and see if he can drive down next weekend instead," she conceded. "I just hate to ask him to change his plans. He'll be as disappointed as I am."

"He might be happy to wait another week if that means he can have you all to himself," her mother observed.

"You're probably right." Patty drummed her fingers on the counter. She had been looking forward so much to their weekend together, and she didn't know if she could take another week of wondering whether their relationship was in some kind of trouble.

But I'll have to, Patty thought, taking a deep breath as she reached for the phone and dialed Jim's college number. Jim would understand how important it was for her to see Jana. Everything would work out fine.

Patty let the phone ring for a full minute, but there was no answer. On one hand she was

12

relieved, but on the other, she almost wished she could get the whole thing straightened out right away. She decided she would call again around dinnertime.

At midnight the next evening, Thursday, Patty was still trying to get in touch with Jim. She sat on her bed and dialed his number. His phone rang. *Five, six, seven, eight*—she counted the rings, then finally replaced the receiver in its cradle and sighed in frustration. That would have to be her last attempt—she had to get some sleep.

Where could he be, anyway? Patty wondered as she pulled her nightshirt on over her head. Even with exams, it was hard to believe Jim had been in the library for twenty-four hours straight.

There were lots of perfectly innocent reasons why Jim might be out so late, Patty told herself. She set the clock radio alarm and switched off the light. But lying in the dark, watching the palm tree outside her bedroom window swaying gently in the breeze, Patty couldn't keep the jealous thoughts that had been bothering her for the past few weeks from creeping back into her mind.

Jim could still be studying for his test or maybe hanging out at a friend's room. *Or, he could be on a date with another girl. . . .*

Restless, Patty rolled over. Since he had started at Pacific in the fall, Jim had never said anything to her about wanting to date other girls.

But maybe now that he had been there for a while, he was having second thoughts about hanging on to his high-school girlfriend.

Deep down, Patty knew Jim still loved her as much as she loved him. When she graduated from Sweet Valley High next year, she planned to attend Pacific, too, so they could be together all the time.

I'll feel better as soon as I see him, Patty decided. *I'm just being paranoid, that's all.* But she couldn't fall asleep for another hour, no matter how many reassurances she gave herself.

Two

"I wish I could help you out," Patty said. "But as you know, I'm already overbooked for this particular weekend."

DeeDee blew her light brown bangs off her forehead, concentrating as she made a last dab with her paintbrush on a T-shirt. Then she laughed. "Don't worry, Patty. I didn't expect *you* to come to my rescue! I'll be able to handle the booth myself."

It was Friday evening, and Patty was at DeeDee's house watching her friend's last-minute preparations for Saturday's crafts fair. Patty, preoccupied over Jim's and Jana's coinciding visits, had arrived to find DeeDee grumbling about a problem of her own. A friend from her civics center design class who had promised to help DeeDee at the fair had come down with the flu.

DeeDee spread the T-shirt on a table to dry.

"There, that makes twenty. All I have to do is iron them so the fabric paint will set. After all this elbow grease, I hope I sell some of them."

"They'll become the latest thing," Patty predicted. "Just don't get swept away by success and forget to save one for me."

"You can have first pick of whatever's left over," DeeDee promised. "Something to wear when you go out tomorrow night with Jim—or with Jana!"

"Don't remind me," Patty said, grimacing. She flopped onto DeeDee's bed. "Jim will be home any minute now. I asked his mom to have him call me here, so I can drive straight over. But it's not going to be much of a reunion because I want to be back home when Jana gets there with her big news."

"He'll be cool about it," DeeDee said, folding a T-shirt and adding it to a stack on the floor.

"Yeah"—Patty tried to convince herself—"of course he'll see it means a lot to me to spend time with Jana after six whole months." She thought of the extra big kiss she would give him so he wouldn't have any doubts about her feelings for him. "Maybe he can come down next weekend, too."

A few minutes later the phone rang, and Patty's heart leapt. Even though their weekend wasn't going to turn out the way they had planned, she couldn't wait to see Jim and feel his arms around her.

16

Patty grabbed the phone off DeeDee's desk and after a breathless hello, told Jim, "I'll be right over."

She gave DeeDee a quick hug and then raced for the stairs. "Have fun, and good luck!" DeeDee called after her.

Patty pulled into the driveway leading up to the Hollises' stucco ranch house, then parked. Before getting out of her parents' car, she checked her reflection in the rearview mirror. Her hair was windswept from driving with the windows down, but she wasn't about to waste time combing it.

The heels of her flat sandals clattering, Patty hurried up the walk to press the door bell. A few seconds later, the door whipped open. "Patty, you nut!" Jim exclaimed, throwing his arms around her in a bear hug. "I swear I just hung up the phone with you. What did you do, fly over here?"

"Something like that," Patty confessed, giggling as Jim squeezed her even tighter. "Would you have preferred I took my time about it?"

"No way." He drew back so he could look at her, his dark brown eyes glowing. "I don't want to waste a minute of this weekend. I've been thinking about you constantly. Well, about you and calculus," he kidded her. "But the exam's over, and now I can focus on you."

17

Patty smiled, stretching on tiptoes to place a soft kiss on her tall boyfriend's lips. Inside, though, she felt a twinge of guilt. Jim didn't want to waste a minute of this weekend. How was he going to feel when she told him there wasn't going to *be* a weekend, at least not the way he expected?

As Jim took her hand and drew her into the front hall and then back to the spacious family room, Patty decided she would wait a little longer before breaking the news. Jana had a long drive from San Francisco and wouldn't reach Sweet Valley for a while yet.

"The house is quiet," Patty observed as she and Jim snuggled down together on the L-shaped sectional sofa.

"My parents are out," Jim explained. He grinned. "It took some work, but I got rid of them. Anything to be alone with you!"

Patty laughed. "Well, here we are. What do you want to do?"

Jim wiggled his eyebrows. "Maybe we could kiss for a couple of hours," he suggested. "Then we could catch our breath and kiss for a couple more."

"That's all you can think about, after you haven't seen me for four weeks?" Patty teased.

Jim's expression grew serious. "No," he said tenderly. "Sure, I want to kiss you. But I also want to talk to you and look at you and hug you . . ."

He put his arms around her, and they sat in silence for a minute, just holding each other. Patty sighed, her cheek pressed against Jim's broad chest. It was going to be hard to leave him so soon.

"I've missed you, Patty," Jim said softly.

"I've missed you, too," she whispered.

"A month is too long to be apart, huh?" he observed. "I'd have made it home sooner, but I've been swamped with work."

"How did the calculus test go, anyway?" she asked.

Jim shrugged. "I think I did OK, but I won't know for sure till I actually see the grade. How about you?" He brushed a strand of hair from Patty's cheek. "How's life in Sweet Valley?"

Patty bit her lip. "Fine. Actually, this weekend . . ." She hesitated.

"What?" Jim prompted. "Do you have a dance recital or something?"

"No, nothing like that. It's my sister, Jana. It turns out she's coming home this weekend, too. It was a real last-minute kind of thing." Patty spoke quickly, keeping her tone light. "Anyway, I tried to call you as soon as I heard to see if you wanted to come down next weekend instead, but you were never at your dorm room."

Jim frowned. "Next weekend? Why? I'm here *this* weekend."

19

"Yeah, well, that's the hard part," Patty confessed, toying with the buttons on Jim's yellow oxford-cloth shirt. "Jana has some big news to tell us—I don't know what. We haven't seen her in six months, since she moved to San Francisco. It looks like we'll be doing a bunch of family stuff. Jana's counting on seeing a lot of me."

"So am I," Jim said, his voice sharp.

Patty blinked. "I'm sorry, Jim, I really am. But Jana's my big sister. I thought you'd understand."

"I do understand," he retorted, his eyes clouding over with angry disappointment. "I understand that your sister's more important to you than I am."

"Don't be ridiculous!" Patty exclaimed, sitting up abruptly. "That's not true at all."

"No? After we haven't seen each other in ages, you tell me you'd rather spend the weekend with Jana than with me. How am I supposed to feel about that?"

"I didn't say that. You're *both* impor—"

Jim cut her off. "It looks like I drove two hours for nothing," he declared. "I might as well have stayed at Pacific and had some fun up there!"

Patty was shocked by Jim's sudden anger. After the warm, loving closeness of a moment before, it was like having a glass of ice water tossed in her face. "Why are you picking a fight with me?" she demanded, hurt.

Jim's eyes narrowed. "*I'm* picking a fight with *you*?" he repeated in disbelief. "You're the one who just canceled our whole weekend because it didn't mean anything to you!"

"You're just being selfish!" Patty cried. "You make it sound as if I *wanted* to back out on you. It wasn't my idea for Jana to come home this weekend! But now I'm starting to be glad she is. I'm starting to think I *would* rather be with her than with you!"

Jim stood up. "That's just fine. Have fun, and thanks for nothing!"

Patty jumped to her feet as well. "I didn't want to argue," she said, her throat constricting as she fought back tears.

"Tell me about it!" Jim shouted. "Who's the one who just spent two hours on the highway for nothing? Why did I even bother?"

"I tried to call you and tell you not to come," Patty said.

"Gee, that was nice of you," Jim snapped.

"At least I tried," Patty said hotly. "Dozens of times, too! Where were you, anyway? You were never home, not even in the middle of the night!"

Jim frowned. "Do I have to check in with you every time I go out?"

"So you *were* out!" Patty cried. "You weren't

21

studying at all! I knew there was a reason you hadn't made it back here lately. If there's another girl, why don't you come right out and tell me?"

The instant the words were out of her mouth, Patty wished she could take them back. It was too late—her secret fear had been spoken.

Jim was stunned and outraged. "Another girl?" he repeated. "Where'd you get an idea like that?"

"You'd think I was seeing someone else if you tried to call *me* and didn't get an answer for days, too!" Patty accused him.

"No, I wouldn't." Jim's voice was cold and surprisingly quiet. "Because I trust you. But it's pretty obvious you don't trust me. Maybe I *should* be dating other girls."

"Go ahead!" Patty picked up a pillow from the couch and hurled it at Jim. "Maybe it's time *I* found a new boyfriend!" Hot tears streaming down her face, she spun on her heel and dashed from the room.

Three

What just happened? Patty wondered, dazed. Half an hour ago she had arrived at the Hollises' with a huge smile on her face; now as she backed the Buick out of the driveway, she was swallowing sobs.

Out on Orchard Road, Patty drove slowly, trying to calm herself by taking deep breaths. As soon as she thought her tumbled emotions were under control, a fresh bout of tears struck. She couldn't help it—the more she thought about her argument with Jim, the more upset and furious she became.

He didn't give me one ounce of credit for doing what I thought was best under the circumstances. He acted as if he was the only person in my life, as if my family didn't matter one bit. Sniffling, Patty pounded her fist on the steering wheel. "How could I know somebody for so long and not realize he was such a self-centered jerk?" she said out loud.

The light at the Ocean Avenue intersection turned red as Patty coasted up to it. Taking advantage of the stop, she fumbled in the glove compartment for a tissue.

As she dabbed the tears on her face, Patty replayed the fight with Jim in her mind. She could hear it all over again, everything he had said—and everything she had said in return. Even though Jim had been unreasonable, Patty knew she had been unfair, too. She had no right to accuse him of cheating on her. To be suspicious just because of a few unanswered phone calls was completely childish and unfair.

So what do I do now? Patty thought. She and Jim had had plenty of spirited discussions in the past, but never an out-and-out shouting match like this. She wondered what was going through *his* mind and whether he was just as confused.

There was only one way to find out: Turn the car around and head back to Jim's house. Patty gripped the steering wheel tightly. When the light changed to green, she hesitated. Then she made a right turn onto Ocean Avenue, continuing toward home. She couldn't face Jim when she was still so worked up. They would probably start yelling at each other all over again. And what if Jim hadn't just been speaking in the heat of the moment? What if he really did want to date other girls?

Patty rolled her window down all the way. The cool night air felt good on her flushed skin. The weekend had gotten off to a rotten start, but she hoped it would improve when Jana arrived home.

All of a sudden, Patty couldn't wait to see her sister. They had been close friends ever since they were little girls, despite the four years' difference in their ages. Patty couldn't count the times she had turned to Jana for support and advice. Jana had never let her down.

She's just the person I need to talk to, Patty realized, her distress easing somewhat. They would have a heart-to-heart talk, just like in the old days when Jana didn't live so far away. Jana was older and wiser—she would know just what Patty should do about her falling-out with Jim. Taking another tissue, Patty wiped her tear-streaked face. Then she sat up in her seat, suddenly eager to be home.

As she drove down Ridgeview toward her family's house, Patty saw a car in the driveway. Jana was already there!

When she entered the driveway, though, she discovered it wasn't her sister's blue VW, but an unfamiliar sports car. *That's funny*, Patty mused as she waited for the electric garage door to lift. *Mom didn't say anything about Jana getting a new car*. It didn't seem very likely; Patty knew her sister didn't exactly make a fortune working for the Bay Area Environmental Coalition.

She entered the house through the side door and immediately heard a hubbub of talking and laughter coming from the front of the house. Patty hurried in the direction of the voices. Her eyes were red, and she had the hiccups from crying, but she didn't care how she looked. She would tell her sister everything the minute she could steal Jana away from their parents.

When Patty reached the entrance to the living room, she froze. At Jana's side stood a tall, broad-shouldered young black man in a crisp uniform, an ear-to-ear grin on his handsome face. Mrs. Gilbert was hugging Jana, laughing and crying at the same time. Mr. Gilbert had just popped the cork from a bottle of champagne.

Patty stared at the scene for a minute. The next thing she knew, Jana was hugging her and dragging her into the living room.

"Patty, you're just in time!" Jana cried. "I'm so happy. I wanted you to be here when I told Mom and Dad, but I gave myself away. I couldn't wait."

Before Jana could say another word, the incredible truth dawned on Patty.

"Ted, this is my little sister, Patty. Pat, I want you to meet Ted Brewster. My fiancé," Jana added, her dark eyes dancing. "We're getting married!"

Patty was struck absolutely speechless. She looked from Jana to Ted in amazement. "Ted, it's—I'm—it's nice to meet you. Congratulations, both of you," Patty finally managed to stutter. She shook Ted's hand awkwardly.

Mr. Gilbert passed around glasses of champagne, with a very small amount for Patty, just enough for a toast. Then he lifted his glass. "You've given us a real surprise," he said to Jana, his deep voice cracking with emotion. "But I can't imagine a nicer one. We love you, Jana. And, Ted, we're proud to welcome you into our family."

Her eyes sparkling with tears, Jana planted a kiss on her father's cheek. Then she and Mrs. Gilbert embraced again. Patty, meanwhile, glanced at Ted and then took a quick sip of the fizzy champagne. She felt as though she had taken a wrong turn on the way home, driven up the wrong driveway, and walked into somebody else's house. Her big sister was announcing she was engaged to some guy that none of them had ever met. It was so unbelievable! It had to be an episode out of "The Twilight Zone."

"OK, everybody, let's sit down," Jana suggested. She ushered Ted to a place on the couch alongside Mrs. Gilbert. Patty collapsed onto the piano bench, her knees weak.

Jana perched on the arm of the sofa next to Ted. Then she smiled across the room at Patty.

27

"Sorry, Patty. We really did mean to wait until you got home before we dropped the bombshell. Ted was cool and collected, but I crumbled the minute I saw Mom and Dad." Ted chuckled, and Jana lifted her hands helplessly. "What can I say, I'm a marshmallow!"

Without intending to, Patty spoke her thoughts out loud. "So *this* is your big news!"

Jana nodded, then looked down at Ted with starry eyes. He gazed back at her affectionately. "You'd never have guessed, huh?" Jana asked.

"Hardly!" Patty was still in a state of shock.

"Well, it sort of surprised us, too," Jana confessed with a soft laugh. "Mom, was it love at first sight with you and Dad?"

Mrs. Gilbert smiled. "Not exactly."

"Not exactly, I should say!" Mr. Gilbert added. "I courted her the old-fashioned way. For two years straight, I visited her every Sunday afternoon, sitting in the front parlor, with her parents for chaperons."

"I'm sure glad times have changed," Jana said, squeezing Ted's hand. "Because we don't want to wait two years."

The engaged couple held each other's gaze for a moment. Then Ted cleared his throat. "I barely had a chance to introduce myself before Jana made our big announcement," he began politely. "I expect you'd like to know a little more about the person your daughter plans to marry."

Mrs. Gilbert smiled. "We'd love to hear a little more about you and your family. Are you from San Francisco originally?"

"No, as a matter of fact, I grew up in Philadelphia," Ted replied. "My father is a school principal, and my mother teaches second grade."

"Where did you get your education, Ted?" Mr. Gilbert asked.

"I graduated from the University of Pennsylvania. Then, since I'd wanted to fly from the time I was a boy, I decided to join the Air Force." Patty could see her parents were impressed with Ted's background and manner. "After I got through training, the service sent me to San Francisco for a year. My assignment there is nearly up," Ted explained.

Mr. Gilbert nodded. "And where will you be stationed next?"

Patty glimpsed a hand-squeeze between Jana and Ted. From the worried, expectant look on Jana's face, she guessed the family was in for another bombshell. Nothing could have prepared Patty for Ted's answer, though. "In three weeks, I leave for West Germany," he announced.

"West Germany?" Mr. and Mrs. Gilbert repeated in unison.

"And I'm going overseas with him," Jana quickly added. "That's what I meant when I said Ted and I don't plan to wait two years. We want to get married in two *weeks*."

29

"Two weeks!" Mrs. Gilbert blurted in astonished dismay. "But, Jana, honey, that's so soon! How on earth can we plan a wedding—and Germany! It's so far away!"

"I know, Mom." Jana reached over to pat her mother's hand. "Getting married and then moving to Europe, all in less than a month! It's a shock for me, too. But Ted and I want to be together. I've never been more sure of anything in my life."

"That's all that really matters, I suppose." Mrs. Gilbert's eyes misted up slightly. "But two weeks! We'll have to start at the crack of dawn tomorrow. I hope Reverend Jacobsen is available to perform the ceremony. And a wedding dress! I suppose Ted will wear his uniform— that's one less thing to worry about. But your father will need a tuxedo or morning coat—what time of day? And where will we have the reception?"

Jana burst out laughing. "Don't worry, Mom! We can do it if we take things one step at a time."

Mr. and Mrs. Gilbert, Jana, and Ted launched into a discussion about how best to contact friends and relatives on such short notice. Patty listened without really hearing them. Her mind was just too full to take in any more information. It was so overwhelming—Jana was getting married and moving to Germany!

Patty stared at her sister as Jana chattered on about the wedding guest list. Jana couldn't take her eyes off Ted and vice versa; it was clear they were very much in love. *And I didn't know a thing about it!* Suddenly, Patty felt almost resentful. Jana had always told her everything in the past. She could recall Jana mentioning during a phone call that she had gone out with an Air Force officer named Ted a few times. But it was a long way from a couple of dates to being engaged! Now some stranger was going to take Jana all the way to Europe.

A wave of hurt and loneliness washed over Patty as she remembered her argument with Jim. Their fight was such a horrible contrast to Jana's and Ted's joyous announcement! One thing was for sure, Patty decided: Telling Jana about the situation with Jim was completely out of the question. It was obvious that Jana only had thoughts for Ted and the upcoming wedding. In fact, everyone was so carried away, they hadn't even noticed the traces of tears in Patty's eyes or her uncharacteristic silence.

It was almost more than Patty could bear. She clenched her teeth, holding back a sob. She had just broken up with her boyfriend, and now in two weeks she was going to lose her only sister, too.

Four

Patty slowly opened her eyes and squinted against the bright morning sunshine. Rolling over, she checked her clock. She had gotten plenty of sleep, but she didn't feel as though she had. Her head ached, and her eyes were itchy and dry, all from crying herself to sleep the night before. Not only that, but she had had a series of bad dreams, mostly about Jim dating other girls.

The worst thing is, the bad dreams started before I even went to bed, Patty thought. She sat up, pulled down the window shade, and then flopped back on her pillow. Thinking about the terrible scene with Jim made her want to start crying all over again.

Patty's eyes were just starting to fill with tears when she heard a knock. Her bedroom door opened a crack, and Jana peeked around it. She was already dressed, and she looked even more radiantly happy than she had the night before. "Morning, Patty. Can I come in?"

Patty sat up and put a pillow behind her back. "Of course."

Jana sat cross-legged at the foot of the bed, facing her sister. "I hope I didn't wake you up. But I really wanted to talk to you, and I couldn't wait any longer."

Patty felt her spirits lift. This was just like old times—she and Jana starting the day with some sisterly gossip. Last night Jana had been too distracted to notice something was bothering Patty. "I wanted to talk to you, too," Patty began. "Last night—"

"Crazy, wasn't it?" Jana broke in. "It must seem so sudden to you and Mom and Dad. Want to know something? It seems sudden to me, too!" Her brown eyes sparkled. "So, I'm dying to know. What do you think of him?"

"Him?" For a second, Patty was tempted to ask Jana whom she was talking about. How had they gotten back onto the subject of Ted when she wanted to talk about Jim? "Well . . ." Patty paused, her head tipped to one side. She barely knew Ted. "He's handsome," she said finally.

"Isn't he, though?" Jana had a dreamy look on her face. "I'll never forget the first time I saw him. He was wearing his uniform, and he looked like something out of a movie. *An Officer and a Gentleman*, you know?"

Patty nodded. She didn't think he was *that* handsome, but there was no need to upset Jana.

Jana looked at her expectantly, and Patty guessed she was waiting for more praise of Ted. "And he seems really . . . nice. And smart," Patty added vaguely.

"He's incredibly special," Jana agreed. "I'm in love with him for so many reasons. And it's important to me that *you* like him, too, Pat. In two weeks he's going to be your brother-in-law. I want you two to be good friends."

"Of course we will be," Patty promised. "I already like him a lot."

Jana bent forward to give Patty an affectionate hug. Then she grew solemn. "That brings me to the real reason I'm barging in on you so early," she said. "I want to ask you something pretty important. It would mean a lot to me to have you right there with me when I get married. Will you be my maid of honor?"

For the first time, it really hit Patty. Her sister was getting married. "Of course I'll be your maid of honor!" Patty said, her voice emotional. "I'd be glad to stand up for you on the happiest day of your life."

"Thanks, Patty!" The two sisters embraced, and Jana sniffled. "What would I do without you?" she asked, wiping away a tear.

"Probably mess up your vows," Patty teased. "This way I'll be standing at the altar to prompt you. I could even hold cue cards if you want."

Jana giggled and rolled her eyes. "I think I can manage 'I do.' "

"We'll see. You never were much at public speaking."

"I suppose you won't be nervous at all at *your* wedding, when you and Jim tie the knot," Jana quipped playfully.

A spasm of pain filled Patty's heart. The way things stood, it was likely she would never even *talk* to Jim again, much less marry him. "Don't count on it," she told Jana, a tremor in her voice. "Jana, I have to tell you—"

"Just a sec," Jana burst out. "I have something to show you. Be right back!"

Patty stared, stunned, as Jana bounced off the bed and dashed for the door. Half a minute later she trotted back into Patty's bedroom, carrying a copy of *Bride* magazine.

"Here, look." Jana flipped rapidly through the glossy pages and stopped at a photograph of an ivory-colored dress shimmering with lace and beads. "Isn't it absolutely beautiful?" she breathed, closing her eyes. "Picture me in it." Patty dutifully pictured Jana in the dress. "I mean, I don't expect to find that dress precisely," Jana admitted, shutting the magazine. "But something along those lines."

"Mmm," Patty mumbled. "It's nice."

Jana glanced at her watch. "Speaking of which, Mom and I are going to Elaine's Bridals this morning—I have an appointment in half an hour."

"What about this afternoon? Could we do something together?" Patty suggested hopefully. "Maybe drive out to the beach. I'd love to spend a little time alone with you. I really want to talk about, you know, things."

Jana shook her head matter-of-factly. "Sorry, but this afternoon's going to be even more hectic than this morning!" she declared. "We've decided to hold the reception here at home, so Ted and I have to find a caterer. Plus we have to book the church and look into flowers. Which reminds me, before we order flowers for the bouquets we need to decide on a dress for *you*. That's why I want you to get up and get your act together. It doesn't look like you'll be ready to come along to the bridal shop, but I could really use your help on the rest of the errands. What do you say?"

Patty's head was swimming. What she really wanted to do was to lie in bed all day and cry. But Jana needed her, if she wanted to get everything done for the wedding. "Sure, I'll help," she said.

"Thanks." Jana jumped to her feet. "I think it'll be fun. Remember when we used to plan what kind of weddings we wanted to have when we were little girls?"

Patty smiled wanly.

"Well, I have to run. See you later this morning, OK?" Jana said, walking to the door.

Patty nodded. "So long. Good luck with the dress."

The door clicked shut behind Jana, and Patty heaved a troubled sigh. Then she climbed out of bed and reached into her closet for her pink-striped bathrobe.

She almost felt like laughing. Who was that woman, anyway? Jana was acting like a different person. The big sister Patty had grown up with was sensitive and kind; but this Jana was so wrapped up in wedding plans she didn't even have time to listen. Patty hadn't been able to get a word in edgewise! Although, she supposed, even if she *had* managed to relate her problems with Jim, Jana would have been too busy to talk to her about it. There would still be a caterer to hire and a dress to buy and a million other things to do.

From her window, Patty saw the Buick leave the driveway with her sister and mother inside. She sighed again, this time a little bitterly. So much for a weekend of sisterly togetherness. Instead, she was going to get dragged along on a bunch of tedious wedding errands.

I might as well have spent the weekend with Jim,

as I'd planned, Patty realized grimly. *Then we would never have broken up!*

Forty-five minutes later Patty stood in her bedroom, drying her hair after a long, hot shower. She rubbed her head vigorously, then tossed the damp towel over the back of her desk chair. She picked up the phone and dialed. After two rings a girl's voice said, "Hello?"

"DeeDee, it's Patty."

"Patty, what's up?" DeeDee asked cheerfully. When Patty didn't answer right away, she prompted, "Is something wrong?"

"Yes," Patty admitted. In a rush, she spilled the news about her fight with Jim, as well as Jana's engagement. "I got my nerve up a few minutes ago to call Jim," she concluded. "I thought we could at least talk things over. But he wasn't home. Maybe he figured I'd call and didn't want to be around for it. Anyway, it's pretty obvious he's not going to apologize to me after all I said."

"Patty, I can't believe so much happened since I saw you last night!" DeeDee exclaimed, concerned. "I'm really sorry. What can I do to make you feel better?"

"Oh, nothing. You're doing it." Patty nervously twirled the phone cord. "I'm just confused. I needed somebody to talk to. Thanks for letting me spill my guts."

"Anytime. You know that," DeeDee said. "I hate to do this, but I've got to run. The crafts fair starts at noon, and I need to be there an hour early to check in and set up my booth."

"I understand," Patty assured her. "Go on. I don't want you to be late."

"Why don't you come by the mall once the fair gets started?" DeeDee suggested. "We can figure out a way to get you and Jim back together."

"I wish I could," Patty told her sincerely, "but I promised Jana I'd help with some of the wedding plans. I am *not* looking forward to it."

"Then I've got an even better idea." DeeDee sounded inspired. "Bill called me awhile ago. He's going surfing today with a buddy of his from out of town, this really great guy named Craig. Craig's sticking around tonight, and the three of us were going to get some dinner and maybe see a movie. Why don't you come along?"

"I don't know." Patty was doubtful. "I should probably stick around at home tonight. My family might do something together. Plus, I don't even know this Craig guy," she said. "I'd feel funny going on a date, not to mention the fact that I'd be the worst company ever, with the mood I'm in."

"Oh, come on," DeeDee urged. "This is just

what you need. Anyway, it wouldn't be a date, just a night out to take your mind off Jim. Craig's an absolute riot. You'll really like him."

Patty was still reluctant. "Thanks anyway, Dee, but I think I'll pass."

DeeDee made one last plea. "After a whole day of it, do you really want to stay home tonight listening to wedding talk and watching your sister and what's-his-name drool over each other?"

Patty had to laugh. "Since you put it that way, I guess I'll have to come along!"

"We'll have a good time," DeeDee promised. "I'll call you when I get home from the fair. We'll probably head out about seven."

"Great. Good luck at the fair, DeeDee. I'll see you." Patty smiled despite herself as she hung up the phone. DeeDee was the best friend in the world; she always came through when Patty needed moral support. But Patty still had doubts about the plans for the evening. She had a feeling nothing and nobody could take her mind off Jim.

Five

"Are you coming or not?" Elizabeth called up the stairs to her twin.

Jessica emerged from her bedroom. She frowned down at Elizabeth, who was wearing shorts and an oversize T-shirt over her new powder-blue bathing suit. Jessica was dressed for the beach, too, but her expression was more like that of someone who had been sentenced to spend a gorgeous Saturday in jail.

Elizabeth looked at her watch. As usual, Jessica was holding up the show. "Todd's waiting in the driveway, Jess. We told Enid and Hugh we'd pick them up around eleven, and it's already quarter past. Are you ready to hit the beach?"

Jessica sat down on the top stair and hugged her knees, undecided. "I'm bored with the beach," she complained.

41

"Bored with the beach?" Elizabeth repeated in disbelief. "I never thought I'd live to see the day my twin sister thought the beach was boring. Are you feeling OK? Should I check your temperature?"

Jessica shrugged and leaned forward to examine her magenta toenail polish. Maybe it wasn't the beach that bored her, she considered. Maybe it was the *people* at the beach. The same old boring people she saw every single day at school—and most of all, the same old boring guys.

"There's going to be a big cookout for Aaron Dallas's birthday. Everyone will be there," Elizabeth reminded Jessica in a persuasive tone. She slung her straw beach bag over one shoulder. "I thought you'd never miss out on an event like that."

"Well, Lizzie, you thought wrong." Jessica put a hand to her mouth to cover a wide yawn. *Aaron Dallas's birthday, big deal!* she wanted to add, but didn't. After all, Aaron was a perfectly nice person. Jessica had nothing against him— hadn't she gone out with him a bunch of times? Maybe that was the problem. She had dated everyone worth dating at Sweet Valley High, and there was absolutely no one new and interesting in the entire student body. What was the point of hanging around at the beach, looking at the same old faces and talking about the same stupid things? It wasn't any fun unless you had a crush on somebody. And, Jessica thought, feeling a little nostalgic and self-pitying, she hadn't *really* liked a boy since she had broken up with A.J. Morgan.

There was a honk from the driveway. "Well, I'm off," Elizabeth announced, her blond ponytail swinging as she turned toward the front door. "Have a good day, however you spend it."

"Ta-ta," Jessica said crabbily.

The door shut behind Elizabeth, and Jessica slowly got to her feet. What *was* she going to do all day, anyway? A Saturday was still a Saturday —her favorite day of the week.

Jessica hopped down the stairs of the modern, split-level house and made her way to the cozy, Spanish-tiled kitchen. Elizabeth had done the breakfast dishes before she left, and the counters were spotless. Hitching herself onto the counter nearest the telephone, Jessica punched her friend Amy Sutton's number. There was no answer. Lila Fowler wasn't home either, Jessica learned from Eva, the Fowlers' housekeeper. It looked as if Elizabeth had been right—everybody *was* at the beach!

Jessica paced around the kitchen, reviewing her options. Suddenly she recalled DeeDee Gordon's remark at lunch a few days earlier. DeeDee had said there was an enormous crafts fair at

43

the mall and that artisans from all over the state would be displaying their work. "Why not?" Jessica asked out loud. It would be a different scene with totally different faces. If all else failed, at least she could spend the day shopping!

"I'm wild about this one," a woman in red-framed sunglasses declared, holding up a white T-shirt painted with a swirling black and turquoise sea-scape design. "I hope it's my size."

"They're all larges," DeeDee informed her. "Most people like to wear shirts big these days."

"And I'm one of them." The woman pulled out an alligator-skin wallet. "How much?"

DeeDee smiled with satisfaction as she wrapped the T-shirt in tissue paper. Another sale! That made six, and the crafts fair had only been underway for an hour. At this rate, she would be cleaned out by midafternoon.

After taking her purchase, the woman lowered her sunglasses and looked at DeeDee over the rims. "You're very talented, dear. I may be back later with my daughter!"

"Great! Thanks," DeeDee said amiably.

As her customer disappeared into the crowd, DeeDee took a moment to rest her elbows on the counter of her booth. "Phew!" she breathed. Part of the mall parking lot had been roped off for the fair, and she had been assigned an outdoor booth rather than one inside. The sun was mercilessly hot, but even so DeeDee was enjoying herself immensely.

She straightened up so browsers could see the shirt she was wearing, as well as those on display. This was the first crafts fair DeeDee had ever exhibited her work at, and she had been more than a little nervous beforehand. Sure, her design teacher thought her work was good, but that didn't mean other people would. It felt great to get so much positive feedback. For the first time, DeeDee was starting to believe she might be able to make a career in art one day.

DeeDee shaded her eyes to look out at the rest of the crafts fair. The only real drawback of being on her own was that she couldn't leave the booth to meet the other artists and check out their work. Other than that, and the fact she was absolutely starving, DeeDee expected to have a good afternoon.

"I don't know," Jessica said, wrinkling her nose. The artist held a mirror for her, and Jessica turned her face to one side, giving her head a little shake to see how the long, dangly earring looked against her hair. It was pretty—made of silver, feathers, and beads—but it wasn't really her style. Besides, she had already bought one pair of earrings, a bracelet, and a scarf at the fair.

"I think I'll have to pass on these," she said, handing the earring back to the artist. "Thanks, anyway."

"Come back if you change your mind," he said, giving Jessica one of his cards.

Boy, is this ever the wrong place to meet a guy! Jessica thought as she wove her way along another row of booths. She had found some wonderful things to wear, but as far as boy-hunting went, the crafts fair had nothing to offer. The male artisans all seemed to be either as old as her grandfather or else skinny, earnest, earthy types in flip-flops and raggedy clothes.

Just then, Jessica glimpsed a familiar face in the crowd. She saw DeeDee Gordon fanning herself with a crafts fair program.

Jessica grimaced. DeeDee wasn't exactly her favorite person in the world. She had never quite forgiven DeeDee for snapping up Bill Chase before she herself got a fair shot at him. But, since DeeDee had spotted her, she supposed it would be rude to completely ignore her.

"Jessica, hi! You're the first person from school I've seen all day," DeeDee commented.

"Tell me about it." Jessica idly fingered one of the T-shirts on the table in front of her. "Everyone else in the universe is at the beach." Then she looked down at the T-shirt she was

46

holding. "Hey, this is wild!" An exotic vinelike pattern had been painted across the short sleeves and around the back of the shirt, giving it an original, striking look. She read the price tag pinned to one of the sleeves and whistled. "Kind of steep for a T-shirt, isn't it?"

DeeDee nodded. "It's more than I'm charging for most of them," she admitted, "but it was a lot more work, too."

"Somebody will buy it," Jessica predicted carelessly. "Well, I'm off."

"Oh, Jessica, before you leave," DeeDee said quickly, "can I ask you a huge favor?"

Jessica frowned. "What?" she asked, her tone less than friendly.

"Would you watch the booth for five minutes while I run and grab something for lunch? The person who was supposed to help me today got sick, and I'm by myself. I could really use a quick break. I promise I'll hurry."

"Well . . ." Jessica was ready to ditch the crafts fair—she had seen enough. But she couldn't think of any legitimate excuse to turn DeeDee down. It wasn't as if she had anyplace else to go. "All right," Jessica agreed grudgingly. "If you're sure you won't be long."

"Thanks a million. Here." DeeDee stepped out of the small booth and then ushered Jessica in. "It's easy. All the T-shirts are priced. If somebody wants to buy one, just make a note

47

of the code number that's written on the tag so I know what's sold. The money's here." DeeDee indicated a metal cashbox under the counter. "Got it?"

"Got it," Jessica said impatiently. "Go ahead."

DeeDee paused to position a tray of hand-lettered business cards more prominently on the counter. "Be right back!" she promised.

Left alone in the booth, Jessica tapped one sandaled foot against the pavement. She wasn't wearing a watch—she never did—but she guessed it wasn't much past one o'clock. It probably wasn't too late to cruise out to the beach and join the gang at the cookout. She had been nuts to think she would meet any appealing guys at the crafts fair.

Then Jessica caught her breath. Approaching her booth at that very instant was one of the most gorgeous men she had ever seen. He had longish black hair and sexy brown eyes. He was wearing faded jeans and a loose linen jacket with the sleeves rolled up.

Unfortunately, it looked as if he was going to pass by without investigating DeeDee's display. *Over here!* Jessica pleaded silently, throwing him an inviting smile. The smile was returned, and Jessica's heart nearly stopped. Forget gorgeous —he had the kind of face you saw once in a lifetime, Jessica thought. Rugged and romantic, he was in his late twenties, Jessica guessed. *He's probably an Italian movie director or a famous artist.* Either way, she was convinced he was the man she had been waiting for.

When he stopped at her booth, Jessica discovered he was even better looking close up. "Hello," he said, his voice as deep and penetrating as his eyes.

"Hi," Jessica breathed, fluttering her lashes as he began examining the T-shirts. "Um, do you see anything you like?" she asked suggestively.

His eyes met hers, and he flashed his smile again. "Actually, I do," he replied. "These shirts are impressive—very unique."

She nodded. DeeDee would want her to make a sales pitch, and in this case Jessica was happy to. "Every design is different," Jessica pointed out helpfully. "And of course, they're hand-painted."

"Wonderful!" He looked closely at a shirt painted in earthy, desert tones. "Do you have any others besides these on display?"

"Let me see." Jessica bent over and fumbled beneath the counter. Sure enough, there was a cardboard carton with half a dozen folded T-shirts inside. "Yes, here are a few more," she said, placing the stack on the counter on top of the tray of business cards. She shook out the top shirt so he could admire it. "What do you think? Would you like to buy one?"

He smiled. "It's nice to meet an artist who's not shy about her work," he observed, an approving look in his smoky eyes. "Let me introduce myself," He held out a strong, tanned hand. "Vincent Delano."

"I'm Jessica Wakefield," she said, tingling as his hand gripped hers.

"It's a pleasure," Vincent said. "Where are you from, Jessica?"

He wants to know if I'm just in town for the crafts fair, she thought. *He wants to ask me out!* "I live right here in Sweet Valley." Jessica hoped her tone made it clear that she was very available.

"So do I," he said. "That makes it easy."

Jessica tilted her head to one side, tossing her hair flirtatiously. "Makes what easy?" she prompted.

Vincent gazed straight into her eyes. "I'd like to make you an offer, Jessica."

Her heart beat faster. *Whatever it is, the answer is yes!* she thought.

"I'm the co-owner of a store in Sweet Valley," he continued. "Do you know Blue Parrot Crafts?"

Jessica raised her eyebrows. "Blue Parrot Crafts?" She was pretty sure she had noticed a new shop by that name on the other side of town. "Sure, I know it."

"We carry hand-made pottery and glass," Vincent told her, "as well as some unique women's clothing and accessories. How would you like to make a big sale?"

Jessica stared at Vincent. Blue Parrot Crafts, a big sale—all of a sudden it made sense. Vincent thought she was the artist! He thought she had designed these crazy T-shirts, and he wanted to buy some for his store.

"Oh, um . . ." Jessica stammered, lowering her eyes and thinking fast. Should she tell him she was just a stand-in for the real artist and risk never seeing him again? Or should she go along with it and cross her fingers that DeeDee wouldn't return and blow her cover?

Jessica never willingly turned her back on an adventure or a great-looking guy, and Vincent Delano definitely qualified. As unobtrusively as possible, Jessica reached under the pile of T-shirts for the tray of cards with DeeDee's name on them. Slipping them out of sight under the counter, she gave Vincent her most captivating smile. "I'd love to make a big sale," she declared.

Vincent laughed. "I like your attitude," he said, leaning forward on the counter so his face was very close to hers. "Why don't I call you sometime soon, and we can talk more about it?"

"Sounds good to me," Jessica agreed with enthusiasm. *I definitely made the right move,* she

51

thought, mentally patting herself on the back. *I should've known it all along. He wants my phone number, not a bunch of shirts.*

Vincent pulled two business cards from his jacket pocket. Handing one to Jessica, he turned the other over. "Your last name again, Jessica? And your phone number, if I may." Jessica was only too happy to give Vincent the information. "Terrific." Vincent pocketed the card, then extended his hand once more. This time, he held Jessica's hand for a few extra moments. "I'll call you very soon," he promised. "I like the idea of displaying some of these shirts at the Blue Parrot. You're a very *gifted* young woman."

"Thanks." Jessica accepted the compliment with only a tiny twinge of guilt. Maybe an element of Vincent's praise belonged to DeeDee; but there was no mistaking the look in Vincent's eyes, Jessica thought. She would have bet a hundred thousand T-shirts that he was more interested in *her* than in her supposed artwork.

"I hope things work out," Vincent said. "I'm sure we can make an arrangement that will satisfy both of us."

"Definitely," Jessica agreed, smiling flirtatiously.

"I have to warn you," Vincent added. "When I see something I want, I'm pretty determined."

Jessica noticed that his eyes were on her, not

on DeeDee's T-shirts. "I like your attitude," she said coyly. "I'm the same way."

Vincent laughed. "Keep thinking like that. You'll be hearing from me," he promised as he strode off to the next booth.

The timing was perfect. No sooner had Vincent strolled away than DeeDee hurried up, carrying a cup of soda and a hot dog. "Thanks so much, Jessica," she said gratefully. "Did I miss much?"

"Not a thing," Jessica answered breezily.

Six

"So, this huge wave came curling over my head from behind," Craig said to Patty. "We're talking *tidal*. I thought, this is it, I'm never going to see land again. I just lay down and wrapped my arms around my surfboard."

"No—really?" Patty was laughing in spite of herself.

"I did," Craig swore solemnly. "Then I just rode the wave like that, peaceful as a baby in a crib. Right, Chase?"

Bill rolled his eyes as he helped himself to another slice of pizza. "Yeah, and I surf standing on my head."

"He does, too," Craig told DeeDee. "This boyfriend of yours is a real nut."

DeeDee giggled. "You're the nut, McCaffrey!"

Patty smiled. Craig's jokes were just what she needed after a long, boring day of being dragged all over Sweet Valley by Jana and Ted. DeeDee had been absolutely right.

I feel a little more like myself, Patty thought as she nibbled half-heartedly at her slice of pizza. The one thing that seemed to be missing was her appetite. Guido's had the best pizza in town, and ordinarily Patty could eat two or three slices, easily. Tonight she could barely manage to eat one.

Patty knew it was because she usually came to Guido's with DeeDee, Bill, and Jim. And even though Craig was a good distraction, something about the whole scene wasn't quite right.

"Enough about our surfing safari," Craig said as he reached for the pitcher of cola. "Word has it you're the Picasso of Sweet Valley High, DeeDee. How did things go at the crafts fair?"

"Great!" DeeDee's brown eyes sparkled. "I sold nineteen T-shirts, all but one. So here." Reaching under the table, DeeDee unzipped her purse and pulled out a rolled-up T-shirt. "This is for you, Patty."

Patty smiled as she unfolded the shirt. "I've been wanting one of these. You sure you don't want to keep it?"

"No way." DeeDee laughed. "With some of the money I made, I can buy more shirts and paint, then start all over again."

Craig whistled in admiration as he examined

the shirt. "This is really something. I guess Chase wasn't just bragging about you, DeeDee."

DeeDee blushed. "It's not so hard," she said modestly. "I learned the basic technique in a design class and then just sort of took off with it on my own."

Bill gave DeeDee a hug. "Don't sell yourself short. You're terrific."

"Yeah, I bet it's not so hard!" Craig wiggled his eyebrows comically. "Give me dots to connect, and I still can't draw a decent picture!"

"Maybe you should stick to surfing," Patty advised, smiling.

"What about you?" Craig asked her. "Do you paint, too?"

"Only my nails!" she joked.

"Patty's a dancer," DeeDee interjected.

"A dancer. You mean like this?" Craig held his arms in a circle over his head, ballet-style.

Patty giggled. "Something like that. I've studied all kinds of dance, including ballet, but I prefer modern and jazz."

"So what do you say?" Craig pretended he was going to drag Patty out of the booth. "Teach me a few steps?"

Laughing, Patty braced herself against the table. "In the middle of Guido's?"

Craig grinned. "Promise me a tango in the parking lot, then."

"You're on," she said, smiling.

A minute later Craig, DeeDee, and Bill were back on the subject of surfing. Turning her wrist slightly under the table, Patty stole a look at her watch. Time had actually passed quickly, she thought. The movie started in half an hour, which meant they would have to leave for the Valley Cinema in ten minutes.

DeeDee had been absolutely right about one thing, Patty reflected. She would have lost her mind if she had had to spend the evening with her family. She had never suspected how much work went into a wedding. The ceremony was only part of it; there was also the rehearsal, then the rehearsal dinner the night before, and a reception after the ceremony. Already Patty had learned enough about throwing a wedding to last a lifetime.

The stress and exhaustion of the day were starting to catch up with Patty. She couldn't wait to sit quietly in the dark at the movies and be alone with her thoughts.

Patty sighed quietly, picking a piece of green pepper off her pizza. All of Craig's jokes hadn't pushed Jim out of her mind for one minute. If anything, being out with Bill and DeeDee only made Patty think about him more. They had double-dated together a zillion times in the past.

Finally the last scrap of pizza was gone, and the pitcher of cola drained. Patty rode to the cinema in Craig's car, with Craig talking a mile a minute, which meant all she had to do was laugh at his remarks. They rejoined DeeDee and Bill in the parking lot and then entered the theater just as the lights were dimming. They grabbed four seats in the rear.

Patty settled back against the worn plush chair. She hadn't heard much about the movie—it had just opened. But DeeDee and Craig had really wanted to see it. *Please let it be funny like Craig,* she hoped. *It can have lots of blood and gore or endless car chases. As long as it's not a love story!*

A few minutes into the movie, Patty gulped. It *was* a love story. She would have given anything to be back at Guido's, but she was stuck. She had to watch, and be reminded of her own lost love with Jim. Suddenly she missed him so much it hurt.

In the movie the main characters became separated by danger and misunderstandings. Mechanically eating the popcorn Craig held out to her, Patty's heart ached for them. *They have to get back together!* she found herself praying. She reminded herself it was just a movie, and told herself not to get worked up about it.

Then she realized what she was *really* hoping was that she and Jim would get back together. The way things had ended between them the night before was just a silly misunderstanding, like the ones in the movie. *If the couple on the screen can acknowledge their mistakes, we can, too,* she thought, smiling in the dark.

By the time the lovers were reunited in a classic Hollywood happy ending, Patty had made up her mind. She would make things up with Jim, no matter what it took. She loved him too much to let him go without a fight. Someone had to make the first move, and she had always been pretty gutsy—she could do it.

The lights came up, and Patty and Craig got to their feet. Patty sniffled discreetly and felt in her purse for a tissue. Craig put an arm around her shoulders and gave her a friendly squeeze. "Hey, we've got a softie here," he told DeeDee and Bill.

"I'm a total cornball when it comes to this kind of movie," Patty admitted, wiping away her tears.

Then she froze, not quite sure whether to believe her tear-misted eyes. Was she seeing things? Had the movie gotten to her that badly?

At the front of the movie theater, turning to head up the aisle in her direction, was Jim. And he wasn't alone. At his side was a beautiful black girl in a short purple dress, a wide purple headband in her dark curly hair. The girl was laughing. Then she said something to Jim, her face very close to his.

Here Patty was, crying over him and wanting to get back together, and the whole time he had been right there in the same movie theater, cuddling up with another girl!

All Patty's tender, hopeful feelings faded as she felt herself becoming angrier by the second. If she had needed any proof that Jim was seeing other girls, here it was! And he didn't even seem to care if all of Sweet Valley witnessed his two-timing. Her eyes blazing, Patty held her ground until Jim saw her, too. His eyes widened with surprise, then his eyebrows met in a dark scowl as he stared at her and Craig.

Patty couldn't bear the thought of a confrontation in a public place. Craig still had his arm casually around her shoulders. Now Patty shoved him abruptly away. Pushing her way through the crowd, she bolted from the theater.

When she reached the sidewalk outside the movie theater, she was panting. For a few seconds there, she had been so hurt and mad she had actually seen stars. Now she was starting to feel a little bit foolish. DeeDee, Bill, and Craig were dashing out of the theater after her.

"Sorry about that," Patty said when they caught up to her. She stared down at her feet, knowing she owed them an explanation, but she couldn't bring herself to talk about what had just taken place. "Um, I think I'd better go home now. I'm not feeling very well."

DeeDee glanced at Bill. "Tell you what, guys," she said, taking charge. "You wanted to see if anybody was hanging out at the Dairi Burger, right? We have two cars, so why don't you go ahead? I'll take your car, Bill, and drive Patty home. Then I'll meet you there later."

The minute Patty was alone in Bill's Mustang with DeeDee, she buried her face in her hands. "I'm sorry, Dee," she sobbed. "You tried to make this a fun night for me, and I blew it."

"No, you didn't," DeeDee assured her, steering the car out of the parking lot. "Don't worry about it."

Patty sniffled. "Did you see Jim and—?" She couldn't even finish her question.

DeeDee nodded. "It's hard to believe. I'd never have suspected anything like that from Jim. I can imagine how you must feel," DeeDee sympathized.

Patty shook her head in confusion. "I'm really starting to think he picked a fight with me on purpose, so he could break up with me. The fact that my sister was visiting was probably just a good excuse."

"Could be," DeeDee conceded. "I don't know, though. That doesn't sound like Jim. Doesn't he usually come right out with whatever's on his mind?"

Patty nodded. Jim had always been straightforward, and dependable, caring, trustworthy, and— She burst into tears again.

DeeDee patted her shoulder. "It's OK, Pat.

When we get to your house, I'll stay with you for a while, so we can talk. Bill can wait for me."

The Gilberts' house was dark and quiet. Patty's mother had left a note for Patty on the kitchen counter. She scanned it rapidly. "My folks took Jana and Ted to some fancy restaurant for dinner," Patty grumbled. "Like they needed to pop more champagne corks and make more sappy toasts!"

DeeDee raised her eyebrows at Patty. "Is it really that bad?"

Patty crumpled the note and tossed it in the trash can. "Oh, it's just my rotten mood talking," she admitted glumly.

"Tell you what." DeeDee opened the refrigerator and scrounged around inside. "Let's go up to your room and have a grouch session. You'll feel better."

A few minutes later, the two girls were seated on Patty's bed with a carton of milk and a plate of chocolate chip cookies between them. DeeDee munched a cookie, listening patiently while Patty tried to put her chaotic feelings into words.

"I'm so confused," Patty confessed, breaking an untasted cookie in two. "Part of me is furious that Jim could treat me this way. I don't think he deserves a second chance. But the other part of me— Oh, DeeDee, I just miss him like crazy." Tears welled up in Patty's dark eyes. "It's been weeks since the last time he was home, and now he's right here in Sweet Valley, and instead of being together and happy, we're apart and I'm miserable."

DeeDee leaned forward to give Patty a comforting hug, nearly knocking over the milk carton. "It's all right," she said, patting her friend's back.

"No, it isn't," Patty said. "Jim's turned out to be a total jerk! How could I have liked him for so long?"

Brrrring. The jangling sound behind her made DeeDee jump. It was the phone on Patty's night table.

The two girls stared at each other. "Do you think it's him?" DeeDee whispered.

"I don't know. Should we answer it?"

"No one else is home," DeeDee reminded Patty. She put her hand on the receiver. When Patty nodded, DeeDee picked up the phone and handed it across the bed.

Patty cleared her throat before saying, "Hello?"

"Is this Patty?"

Patty knew the voice on the other end of the line as well as she knew her own. "It's Jim," she hissed at DeeDee, lowering the receiver and pressing it against her shirt so Jim couldn't hear. "What should I do?"

"Be strong," DeeDee advised. "Don't let him

walk all over you. You deserve to know the truth. Stand up for yourself."

Patty uncovered the mouthpiece. "Yes, it's me," she said, trying as hard as she could to keep her voice steady.

"Patty, I don't know what's going on with you," Jim began, sounding tense and nervous. "But at the movies just now—it's not what it looked like—"

Patty cut him off. "I can't believe you, Jim Hollis," she shouted into the phone. "Do you expect me to buy any old line you toss at me? Do you think I'm that gullible?"

"Patty, it's not a line. That girl is—"

"Don't waste your breath on more lies!" Patty burst out. "You can't defend yourself. You were on a date, and you know it. It sure didn't take you long to forget me!"

"Forget you?" Jim snapped, his voice rising. "Look who's talking. How long have *you* been seeing somebody behind *my* back?"

Patty's fingers tightened around the phone. "How dare you accuse me of cheating," she said, outraged. "You're just trying to twist things around because you got caught!"

"The only thing I'm guilty of is stupidity," Jim declared hoarsely. "I was dumb enough to think I could have a civil conversation with you!"

"Well, don't make the same mistake again. I

never want to talk to you again!" Leaping to her feet, Patty sprang toward the night table and slammed down the receiver with all her might.

"Oh, Patty," DeeDee gasped, her hand over her mouth.

"It's over. It's really over." Patty threw herself on the bed and buried her face in the pillow.

DeeDee sighed. "What are you going to do now?"

Patty sat up. "There's nothing to do," she said honestly. "Dee, you might as well go on to the Dairi Burger. I'll be OK."

"Are you sure?"

"Yeah." Patty squeezed her friend's hand. "I want to be by myself for a while. I've got a lot to think about."

"Well, I'll call you tomorrow," DeeDee promised.

Patty walked DeeDee out to Bill's car, then slowly climbed the stairs back up to her bedroom. She turned out the light and sat on her bed in the dark. Patty could feel the warm and humid air coming in through her open window. In the distance, thunder rumbled and heat lightning flickered.

I did the right thing tonight, giving Jim a piece of my mind, Patty thought. *Maybe I'm lucky I realized what an idiot he was before things got too seri-*

ous between us, before I actually went to Pacific College next year to be with him!

The rain-scented breeze brushed against her cheek, cooling her flushed skin. The air smelled good, fresh and full of life. Suddenly Patty was reminded of a night when she and Jim had driven up to Las Palmas Canyon the summer before, for a picnic on the rocks above the gorge. A summer thunderstorm had caught them, and they had gotten thoroughly drenched. But instead of being upset, they had laughed and danced around in the rain like a couple of little kids. Jim had picked her up in his arms and twirled her around and around and around. . . .

A fat tear slid down Patty's cheek. *I can't be mad at him,* she thought. *I can't hate him because I still love him.*

A cold, lonely ache stole into Patty's heart. Remembering that night at the canyon, and so many other special times, made her wonder. She had never been in love before—Jim was her first serious boyfriend, and she thought she knew him inside and out. All of a sudden he had turned into a stranger. How could his feelings for her have changed so suddenly?

A flash of headlights sliced through the dark and drizzle. Off to the side of the house, Patty heard a car's engine in the driveway. She was glad her bedroom light was out. Her family would see her purse and jacket in the kitchen and figure she was home and already asleep, so she would be spared talking to anybody.

Lighthearted voices mingled downstairs, and Patty heard Jana's happy laughter. The contrast between her own sorrow and Jana's joy was almost more than Patty could stand.

Right now, Jana and Ted are together, both happier than they've ever been, Patty thought, closing her eyes against a new flood of tears, *while I'm having the worst night of my entire life.*

Seven

Patty sniffed the air, her stomach growling. After barely touching the pizza at Guido's the night before, she was ravenous, and it smelled like the usual big Sunday breakfast was in the works. Bacon and eggs and cinnamon coffee cake . . .

As great as it smelled, breakfast wasn't enough to get Patty out of bed. She rolled over, trying to convince herself she wasn't the least bit hungry. Right now she bet that her parents, Jana, and Ted were all in the kitchen, chatting about the wedding, and she couldn't face that topic, not yet.

Patty had just closed her eyes for a catnap when the phone rang, startling her so that she nearly fell out of bed. Her eyes like saucers, she stared at the beige phone on the night table. She lay there, paralyzed, remembering her conversation with Jim the night before. What if it was him?

After three rings, someone picked it up downstairs. "Patty!" Mrs. Gilbert called up the stairs. "Are you awake? Phone's for you."

"OK, Mom!" she yelled back. It had to be Jim, she thought, a feeling of panic almost overwhelming her. Maybe he was calling to apologize or to say that he thought they deserved another chance together. Patty sat up and picked up the receiver gingerly. For a long second, she couldn't speak. Then she managed a wobbly, hopeful, "Hello."

"Hi, Patty," said a sunny voice. "It's Liz. I hope I'm not calling too early, but I wanted to reach you before you headed out for the day."

Patty felt as though she had a big lump in her throat. Of course Jim wasn't going to call her. She had told him flat out she never wanted to talk to him again, and no doubt the feeling was mutual. "Oh, no, it's not too early at all." Patty tried to sound a little more upbeat. "What's going on?"

"Well, it's about our interview tonight. I was wondering if we could meet at eight o'clock instead of seven. Is that all right with you?" Elizabeth asked.

Patty had forgotten all about the interview. For a split second, she considered canceling it. But she had promised Liz, and it wouldn't be right to back out on her and mess up her new column for *The Oracle*.

"Eight's fine," Patty said listlessly.

"Good," Elizabeth said. "This way you'll have an extra hour to organize your thoughts. I can't wait to hear about your plans for the future."

Your plans for the future. A wave of misery washed over Patty. A few days ago, her plans for the future had been set: She was going to study liberal arts and major in dance at Pacific College, where she and Jim would be together. Patty clutched the phone tightly, trying to hold back tears.

"Patty, are you still there?" Elizabeth asked, obviously puzzled by the lack of response.

"Yes," Patty answered, her voice breaking.

"Patty, what's the matter? I thought you'd be on top of the world this morning after seeing Jim. Is something wrong?"

"Everything's wrong," Patty wailed.

"Do you want to talk about it?" Elizabeth asked, concerned.

Patty managed to get a few words out. "I'm sorry, Liz, but I'm on the verge of bawling like a baby for about the hundredth time this weekend."

Elizabeth thought for a moment. "Tell you what. Why don't you come over now?" she suggested. "Not for an interview necessarily—just to talk. I was about to have brunch, and then I'm planning to sit out back by the pool. I'm a good listener, you know," Elizabeth said.

Patty knew there was no one more genuinely kind and sympathetic than Elizabeth Wakefield. Perhaps talking to her would help her sort out her feelings. "OK, Liz, you're on. I'll be over in half an hour." Patty laughed weakly. "Get the tissues ready!"

The water in the Wakefields' swimming pool sparkled in the bright sunshine. On the far side of the deck, Jessica was lying on a lounge chair, her face turned toward the late morning sun. Elizabeth had waited to eat until Patty arrived. Now, sitting at the picnic table, the two girls dug into a brunch of fresh pineapple, bagels, and cream cheese.

"Thanks for inviting me over," Patty said, giving Elizabeth a grateful smile. Although Patty's eyes were a little red, Elizabeth was glad to see her looking better than she sounded on the phone a short while ago. "And thanks for feeding me. This hits the spot."

"Fresh pineapple is my favorite," Elizabeth agreed, spearing a slice with her fork. "And I love Sunday mornings. No matter how much homework I have, I always treat myself to at least an hour by the pool."

"I wouldn't be able to limit myself to an hour,"

Patty said. "If we had a pool, I'm sure I'd make a career of lying by it!"

"Like some people I know," Elizabeth said, winking and nodding in Jessica's direction. "So, Patty." She hesitated, not wanting to seem as if she were prying. "Do you want to talk about it? Is it Jim? I promise," she added lightly, "this is off the record and not part of my interview for *The Oracle!*"

Patty managed a very small smile, but the heartsick look in her eyes told Elizabeth she had guessed correctly. Patty took a deep, steadying breath. "After I talked to you on Wednesday," she began, "I found out that my sister was coming home from San Francisco this weekend, too. I decided to try and change my plans with Jim so I'd be free to do stuff with my family, but I couldn't reach him at college before he left. I tried to explain the situation to him Friday night when he got here, but he just blew up. He accused me of putting my sister before him, and then *I* said all this jealous stuff like 'Where were you when I tried to call?' and so on. We had a huge, and I mean *huge*, fight." Patty's chin trembled slightly. "Basically, we broke up then and there!"

Elizabeth winced. "But, Patty, people often say things they don't mean in the heat of the moment. Have you tried to talk to Jim? Maybe it's not as bad as you think."

Patty shook her head. "No, it's *worse*. Last night, I went to the movies with DeeDee and Bill, and a friend of Bill's from Santa Monica, Craig. Guess who was at the exact same movie?"

"Jim?"

"Jim," Patty confirmed, "with a date."

Elizabeth raised her eyebrows. No wonder Patty was hurting so badly!

Patty, meanwhile, had bent her head, pretending to concentrate on spreading cream cheese on a bagel. Elizabeth looked away and watched her golden retriever, Prince Albert, chase a butterfly on the lawn.

"I woke up this morning hoping it was all a bad dream," Patty said softly. "Jim's meant the world to me for so long. How could that have changed so fast?"

Elizabeth sighed, wishing she knew the answer. She felt for Patty, one hundred percent. Her own relationship with Todd was currently strong and happy, but that hadn't always been the case. They had had their share of romantic complications in the past. When Todd moved to Vermont, he had fallen in love with another girl, and Elizabeth had thought she would never care for anyone again. Then she met Jeffrey French, and for a while it looked as if their relationship was meant to last. But when Todd moved back to Sweet Valley, Elizabeth realized after much soul-searching that she had never

73

stopped loving him. She knew that being in love was never easy.

"You and Jim said a lot of terrible things to each other, but that doesn't mean things are over for good between you," Elizabeth gently advised. "Take last night at the movies. You saw Jim with another girl, and he saw you with another guy, right?"

Patty nodded. "And when he called later, he had the nerve to accuse me of seeing other guys behind his back! I hardly even *know* Craig—he's just a friend of Bill's."

"Exactly. He jumped to conclusions about you, just as you did about him," Elizabeth pointed out.

"Yeah, but Jim knew this girl, I could tell," Patty argued. "The way they were talking to each other, it was pretty clear they weren't exactly strangers."

"Maybe not, but she could just be a good friend." Elizabeth paused to take a bite of her bagel. "You know, the same thing once happened with Todd and me. He saw me in a restaurant with another guy, Nicholas Morrow. Nicholas and I are very close friends, and that's it. Still, it looked suspicious to Todd, and he assumed the worst."

Patty tipped her head to one side, a wisp of her dark hair falling across her forehead. Her expression was half-skeptical, half-hopeful. "Do

74

you think something like that was going on with Jim and that girl? Do you think I just assumed too much?"

"I don't know," Elizabeth admitted. "But we know *he* at least made a mistake about you and Craig. Your date with Craig was perfectly innocent—it's possible Jim's was, too. In any case, you should make sure."

"You mean, talk to him," Patty said, folding her arms across her chest.

Elizabeth nodded. "Definitely. Sometimes it's hard to be the one to swallow your pride." She laughed ruefully. "Believe me, I know! But you owe it to yourself, and to Jim, to find a way to talk all this over and really set things straight. Otherwise, you'll never know if you should have broken up or not."

For a few moments the two girls sat in silence while Patty mulled over Elizabeth's words. "You're right, Liz," she said finally. "I don't have anything to lose. Just something to gain, if it turns out I'm wrong about Jim."

"You won't regret it," Elizabeth promised.

"I'll call him as soon as I get home," Patty added with determination. "Now, how about that interview?"

"You sure you're up for it?" Elizabeth asked, smiling.

"It'll psych me up for a talk with Jim," Patty said, leaning back in her chair "Fire away!"

*　　*　　*

Waving from the car window to Elizabeth, Patty backed the Buick out of the Wakefields' driveway. Talking to Elizabeth had helped even more than Patty expected, mostly because everything Elizabeth said made so much sense. It *was* easy to have a misunderstanding. Maybe she and Jim had just been very lucky never to have anything like this happen before.

Just then, Patty had an inspiration. She wouldn't wait to call Jim when she got home; she would drive over to his house right now! Face-to-face with Jim, she couldn't chicken out. She would have to say what was really on her mind and in her heart.

So instead of turning onto her own street, she continued half a mile farther to Jim's neighborhood. *Maybe this won't be so hard*, Patty thought. In the bright sunshine, it was difficult to believe that things wouldn't turn out right. She held her breath as she rounded a bend in the road and the Hollises' yard came into view. Two people were on the emerald-green lawn tossing a Frisbee back and forth. Patty blinked, for the second time that weekend wishing she didn't have to believe her eyes. Jim was playing Frisbee with the same girl he'd been with at the movies.

Slouching in the driver's seat, Patty accelerated, praying Jim wouldn't recognize the car as she sped by. Once she was past the low stucco house, she checked the rearview mirror. Jim was laughing, and shouting something to his friend. He seemed to be having a great time.

What would Liz say now? Patty wondered grimly. *Would she still think Jim was innocent?*

Patty drove around the block, heading back toward her own house. She frowned when she reached home: Ted's car was still in the driveway. She had hoped the happy couple would have already left for their day's errands.

The instant Patty stepped into the house, Jana ambushed her. "Patty, there you are! Where did you rush off to in such a hurry?"

"Just to a friend's house for brunch," Patty answered defensively. "Anything wrong with that?"

"Of course not!" Jana laughed. "But you're back just in time. Ted and I are on our way to the mall, and I want you to come along. You know the dress we picked out for you yesterday at Bibi's? They said they could do a fitting today."

Patty shrugged her shoulders. At the moment she didn't care what she did. She would try on as many dresses as Jana wanted. "Fine. Let's go," she said.

Ted, Jana, and Patty drove to the mall with the radio in Ted's car blasting and the windows down. But Patty didn't feel like having fun. As far as she was concerned, the day was ruined. Patty slumped in the backseat, not bothering to contribute to Jana and Ted's conversation about California's wonderful weather and how different it was going to be living in Germany. How could she care about something as trivial as the weather when Jim had ditched her for another girl?

Halfway to the mall, Jana turned around in her seat and gave Patty an inquiring look. "You're so quiet, Patty," she observed. "Is something on your mind?"

Now, of all times, Jana was finally noticing that she was upset! Patty thought. She didn't want to go into details of her personal life in front of Ted, whom she barely knew. So, avoiding Jana's gaze, Patty tried to sound casual. "Nothing's wrong," she said quietly. Then she thought she would hint at the truth. Perhaps Jana would pick up the hint and ask to have a sister-to-sister talk when they got back from the mall. "Jim and I had an argument, that's all," she added.

Jana glanced at Ted, and the smile returned to her face. "Don't worry about it, Patty," she said breezily, planting a kiss on Ted's cheek. He didn't take his eyes off the road, but Patty saw him grin. "Ted and I have little tiffs all the time. Believe me, they don't mean a thing. Anyhow, once you see yourself in that gorgeous dress at Bibi's you'll forget all about it!"

In the backseat, Patty's jaw dropped. *Little tiffs . . . forget all about it?* Jana had to be kidding!

Not observing Patty's reaction, Jana launched into a description of the maid-of-honor dress for Ted's benefit. "It's cornflower blue with tiny white flowers on it, and it has a scooped neckline and little puffed sleeves. She'll look like a princess in it."

Patty almost asked Ted to pull over to the side of the road to let her out of the car. How could her own sister be so insensitive? How could she think that some dumb dress was more important than Patty's relationship with Jim?

I just want this day to be over. Patty thought, closing her eyes. She couldn't wait for Monday when she could go back to school and dance class, get away from the two lovebirds, and try to forget that this terrible weekend had ever happened!

Eight

"Jessica, would you get the basil and oregano?" Mrs. Wakefield asked, quickly scanning the recipe in front of her.

"Heads up, Mom!" Jessica grabbed the jars from the spice rack and pretended she was going to toss them across the kitchen.

"Don't you dare." When she smiled, Alice Wakefield looked almost as young as her sixteen-year-old daughters.

"You're no fun," Jessica teased, handing over the jars.

"Hey, cooking dinner is serious business," Mrs. Wakefield protested as she stirred the herbs into the tomato sauce simmering on the stove.

"Tell me about it," Jessica said, munching on a carrot she had snitched from the salad bowl.

"Somebody should," Elizabeth piped up from the dining table.

Jessica feigned astonishment. "Liz, are you trying to say that I don't help out with dinner or something?"

Ordinarily Mrs. Wakefield, an interior designer, worked until six o'clock, so Jessica and Elizabeth took turns making dinner. Jessica, however, was a genius at coming up with excuses, and half the time she got Elizabeth to cover for her.

"Who, moi? Insinuate something unkind about you, dear sister?" Elizabeth grinned. "Never."

"I'm here tonight, aren't I?" Jessica pointed out.

"And what a help you've been, too," Mrs. Wakefield kidded.

"I'm hurt, Mom," Jessica said, trying not to smile. "I put a lot of effort into getting those spices." She sighed dramatically as she sauntered out of the kitchen. "I guess my talents just aren't appreciated here—"

Then the phone rang, and Jessica stopped. Nine times out of ten it was for her—usually either Lila or Amy calling to gossip.

Elizabeth answered the call. She held the receiver out toward her twin. "Jess, it's for you. A guy," she added in a whisper.

Jessica stifled a yawn. "Maybe it's time we get an unlisted number," Jessica said, "to discourage the undesirables."

Elizabeth rolled her eyes as she handed the

phone to her twin. "Hello, this is Jessica," she said in a bored voice.

"Jessica, I'm glad I caught you. This is Vincent Delano from the Blue Parrot Shop."

Vincent! Jessica almost dropped the phone. It was Tuesday, three days since the crafts fair, and she had practically given up on hearing from him. Usually, when Jessica gave a guy her phone number he called in a matter of hours.

"Vincent, hi," she said eagerly. Then Jessica noticed that Elizabeth was lingering within earshot. She hadn't told her twin about the episode at the fair, and she didn't plan on it. Elizabeth would definitely not approve of her letting Vincent believe she had painted the T-shirts and taken the credit away from DeeDee.

"Just a moment," Jessica murmured into the mouthpiece. Untwisting the tangled phone cord, she stretched it as far as it would go, out of the kitchen and into the dining room. "It's great to hear from you, Vincent," she purred when she was confident of her privacy. "What's up?"

"Well, I've been thinking about you a good deal since we met at the crafts fair on Saturday," he began, his voice deep.

A chill of excited satisfaction ran up Jessica's spine. It was exactly the way she had imagined it. Vincent wasn't calling about any old T-shirts: he had *her* on his mind! "I've been thinking about you, too," she said warmly.

"Then you haven't forgotten our conversation?" Vincent asked.

"How could I forget it?" Jessica replied. "It was the highlight of my day at the fair!" That much was certainly true.

"Good," Vincent declared. "Then no one else offered to buy a quantity of your T-shirts for resale, I hope?"

"Um, no, no one else did." Jessica was thrown somewhat by the turn the conversation was taking. Didn't Vincent want to ask her out?

"Then you're open to an offer from the Blue Parrot?" Vincent persisted.

Jessica bit her lip. "Uh, sure. I guess."

"Fantastic," Vincent said enthusiastically. "How soon will you be free to meet with me and Cassie, my partner? I told her about your work, and she's eager to see it for herself."

"How soon?" Jessica repeated, her mind going blank. *Good question!* she thought. *Maybe when I get struck by lightning, then I'll turn into an artist!*

"I'm aware you may not be prepared right now, especially if you sold most of your shirts at the fair," Vincent added.

"I sold them all," Jessica fibbed quickly, hoping Vincent would drop the T-shirt idea and move on to more interesting subjects, like taking her out for dinner or dancing.

"I'm not surprised. Your work is superb!" Vincent praised her. "Well, do you think you could paint three or more sample designs between now and, say, a week from today? Then, with Cassie's approval, perhaps we could come to an agreement about selling your T-shirts at the Blue Parrot."

For a long moment, Jessica was silent as she racked her brain for a way out of this particular situation. It looked as though she had only two alternatives: confess to Vincent that she had lied to him at the fair or go along with his proposal.

And if she admitted she couldn't even paint her fingernails without making a mess, she had a feeling she would never hear from Vincent again. That was the last thing she wanted to happen! He was the first exciting guy she had met in ages. Sparks had really flown between them, and there was no way she was going to waste that chemistry.

"Sure," Jessica agreed at last, trying her best to sound confident and artistic. "A week from today would be fine." *Now that the business part of this conversation is over, Vincent is sure to ask me out!* she thought, smiling.

"I'm sorry it can't be sooner," Vincent said.

Jessica sighed happily. Now this was more like it! "Me, too," she said softly.

"But I know you're worth waiting another week for."

"You'd better believe it," Jessica said meaningfully.

"Well, until next Tuesday at three o'clock, then," Vincent confirmed. "Thank you, Jessica."

Still waiting for Vincent to ask her for a date, Jessica didn't realize at first that he had hung up the phone. Then an unsettling possibility struck, along with the sound of the dial tone. Maybe Vincent didn't want a date with Jessica Wakefield after all. Maybe he just wanted DeeDee Gordon's T-shirts!

Either way, she had an appointment at the Blue Parrot in one week, and she had to show up with some T-shirts. She ran one hand through her hair. *What have I gotten myself into now?*

The same night at the Gilberts', Patty and Jana were helping their mother prepare dinner. Ted had returned to the Air Force base on Sunday, but Jana was staying at home until the wedding, having already quit her job. Patty thought Ted's departure would be a relief; she hoped Jana would settle down now and be more like her old self. Instead, Jana was more absorbed than ever in the wedding plans. For four days straight, no one in the family had talked about anything else.

At the dinner table as Patty, her parents, and Jana helped themselves to lasagna and tossed salad, the topic of conversation was the menu for the reception. Patty's mood, which had been so good after dance class, turned sour. She was so sick of discussing the wedding!

"What do you think, Dad?" Jana asked Mr. Gilbert. "The caterer needs a decision tomorrow. Which sounds better to you—chicken, veal, or some kind of fish?"

Pizza, Patty felt like suggesting.

Predictably, her father caught the question and tossed it back. "You choose, sweetie. It's your party!"

"I'm leaning toward chicken," Jana admitted. "But, Daddy, there's one thing you have to take care of. Don't forget to order the wine and champagne. The caterers don't cover alcohol."

"Don't worry, I'm on top of it," Mr. Gilbert promised with a wink.

"The only thing I regret is not having time to get printed invitations," Jana said, sighing. "But it wasn't so hard making phone calls, was it, Mom?"

"It was fun," Mrs. Gilbert declared. "Everyone was so surprised and excited!"

Jana stopped talking just long enough to take a bite of lasagna. Then she turned to Patty. "Of course I want you to bring Jim to the wedding, Patty," she said brightly. "Do you want me to call him, or can I trust you with the task?"

Patty looked down at her lasagna. "I'll call him," she said, a hint of strain in her voice.

Jana didn't seem to notice. The wedding chatter continued unabated: Patty was the only one who didn't contribute. She didn't trust herself to speak. She still hadn't told her family that she and Jim had broken up. She didn't know how to broach the subject, with everyone fussing nonstop about the wedding. They were all so happy, and they figured Patty was, too.

For a few days, Patty had kept up the hope that her relationship with Jim wasn't over forever. On Sunday afternoon when she, Jana, and Ted got back from the mall, Patty had remembered Elizabeth saying that the whole thing could have just been a big misunderstanding. Doing her best to forget the memory of Jim and the girl she had seen with him twice, Patty phoned his house. Mrs. Hollis had answered, and she told Patty that Jim had already left to go back to college. Patty had decided to try him at school the very next day.

But when Patty called Jim's dorm room several times on Monday and again that evening, he hadn't been at home. It was like last week, all over again, she thought. Patty was convinced that Jim was involved with somebody else and that he was purposely avoiding her calls. *And Jana wants me to call Jim and invite him to the wedding!* she thought, sighing over the irony. She poked at a piece of spinach on her salad plate. Then she realized her mother was talking.

"Jana," Mrs. Gilbert said, glancing across the table. "Your Aunt Marlene called today and said that she wanted to give you a bridal shower."

"A shower!" Jane exclaimed. "Mom, we don't have time for a shower, with the wedding less than two weeks away."

"There's plenty of time," Mrs. Gilbert said matter-of-factly. "This weekend, for example. How about Saturday afternoon? Marlene thought that would be a good time."

"But, Mom, I don't want her to go to any extra trouble," Jana said earnestly.

"It's no trouble," Mrs. Gilbert insisted. "She wants to do it. It may be rushed, but no daughter of mine is getting married unless it's done properly, and that includes a bridal shower! Besides, Patty and I will help. Right, honey?"

Patty cracked a weak smile. "Of course, Mom. You and Aunt Marlene can count on me."

"I know we can, baby," Mrs. Gilbert said. "Jana, right after dinner why don't you give me a list of the friends you want to invite? Your cousins and Marlene can start making calls. Marlene thought she'd do something simple—tea and cookies, along those lines. Patty, you could help with the shopping."

Her mother looked at her, and Patty mustered up a small measure of enthusiasm. "Sounds good, Mom. Sure, anything you say."

Mrs. Gilbert smiled, and Patty smiled back, her face feeling unnaturally stiff. *All this good cheer is such an effort when you don't feel cheerful!* Patty thought. It wasn't as if anybody really wanted her opinion anyway. Everyone was talking *at* her, but no one was talking *to* her, listening to her.

She knew her mother was only trying to make her feel included, though. Suddenly something occurred to Patty. *Maybe if I try to throw myself into all the wedding activities I'll get distracted and forget about Jim.*

She sighed. No, it would never work. All the talk about love and marriage only made her miss Jim more. She wasn't sure how much more she could take.

Nine

"I'm busy on Friday," Jessica said, breezily brushing off Jim Daley's hopeful question. "Thanks anyway."

Jim Daley, she thought as she turned her back on him to scan the crowded cafeteria. *He's a perfect example of what's wrong with Sweet Valley guys.* He had taken her to a dance once, and they had had a decent time. He was cute enough—but he was so boring, it was sad. *I'd rather go on a date with Chrome Dome Cooper,* Jessica thought, giggling as she pictured herself at the Dairi Burger with the bald principal of Sweet Valley High, the most unromantic male she had ever met.

As she crossed the cafeteria, she spied who she was looking for—DeeDee Gordon. She was glad DeeDee was alone at a table with Patty Gilbert. As much as possible, Jessica wanted to keep her latest scheme to herself. She wove her way among the lunch tables, her mint-green jersey miniskirt swinging against her slim, tanned legs.

DeeDee and Patty were sitting with their elbows on the table and their faces close together, deep in conversation. They didn't notice Jessica until she pulled up a chair across from them. "Hi, DeeDee, Patty. How're you doing?" she asked.

Patty's slender black eyebrows lifted in friendly surprise. "Hi," she replied.

"Hi, Jessica," DeeDee said, looking somewhat startled as well. "What's up?"

"Oh, nothing." Jessica shrugged casually. "Just thought I'd stop by and say hello. I haven't bumped into you since Saturday at the mall, DeeDee. How did the rest of the crafts fair go?"

"Fantastic," DeeDee answered. "Would you believe I was cleaned out? I sold all but one of the shirts."

"And she gave that one to me," Patty said, smiling.

"That's fantastic," Jessica observed cheerfully. Inside she cursed her luck. *There goes that possibility!* She had been about to offer to buy a bunch of T-shirts from DeeDee, saying she wanted to give them away for Christmas presents. Then she could have taken DeeDee's shirts to the Blue Parrot. As soon as Vincent asked her out, of course, she would have admitted that someone else had painted them. At that point he wouldn't care about Jessica's little white lie because he would be completely infatuated with her.

Rats, Jessica thought, annoyed. *And it was such a good plan! Now what?*

"Well, the shirts really were beautiful," Jessica said, killing time while she waited for another plan to come to her. She pictured DeeDee's shirts in her mind. When you came right down to it, they were just splashes of paint on men's white undershirts. How hard could it be to make something like that?

I'll paint my own T-shirts! Jessica decided. *Then, not only will I impress Vincent, I'll make a few bucks at the same time.* "You know, DeeDee," Jessica continued, leaning forward in her chair, "I liked your T-shirts so much, I was thinking about painting a few of my own."

DeeDee glanced at Patty. Then she smiled at Jessica. "I didn't know you painted, Jessica."

"Well, I don't really," Jessica admitted, struggling to keep her tone sweet. "I thought it might be fun to paint one for my mother, though, for her birthday."

"Well, sure, if you want, but—"

"What kind of paint do you use? Where do you buy it?" Jessica interrupted.

DeeDee seemed confused by Jessica's abrupt

manner. "What kind of paint? Well, it's fabric paint, of course. I buy it at Ferriter's Design Supply, and the brand I like best is . . ."

Jessica grabbed a paper napkin. "Do either of you have a pen?"

DeeDee pulled a pen out of her shoulder bag and handed it to Jessica.

"What brand was that again?" Jessica asked, jotting it down as DeeDee repeated the name. "And you said Ferriter's?"

DeeDee nodded. "Yeah, on Main Street. They should have everything you need. And you can buy regular white T-shirts anywhere. I usually buy men's 'cause people like them large. But, Jessica, it's not as easy as—"

"Thanks, DeeDee," Jessica chirped, getting to her feet. "Can't wait to give this new hobby a shot. So long."

Turning on her heel, Jessica hurried off, oblivious to DeeDee's and Patty's flabbergasted expressions. She planned to take the Fiat and drive to Ferriter's right after cheerleading practice. *I can't believe I'm going to all this trouble just for a date,* Jessica thought. *Talk about desperate! It just goes to show what a girl's forced to do to keep her social life alive in Sweet Valley these days!*

"Was that weird, or what?" DeeDee asked Patty when Jessica was out of earshot.

"I didn't think Jessica was the artsy type," Patty admitted.

DeeDee rolled her eyes. "She's not, unless some amazing transformation took place since art class last year. We did a unit on sculpture, and everyone had to make a sculpture of somebody else in the class. Jessica did Charlie Markus, but her piece looked more like Mickey Mouse!"

Patty giggled. "Sounds like you'd better watch out at the next crafts fair, Dee. You might have some competition."

Taking a bunch of grapes from her lunch bag, DeeDee shook her head. "You never know in the art world," she joked. "Abstract is in, after all."

Patty bit into her egg salad sandwich. Jessica had been a nice distraction, but now her thoughts returned to the situation at home. DeeDee seemed to read her friend's mind. "Are things really that bad, Patty?" she asked.

Patty put the sandwich back down on her plate. She still wasn't very hungry. "They're not that terrible," she acknowledged, sighing. "I mean, I can't say it's bad when everybody but me is flying high. I just feel like I've suddenly become an orphan. I need someone to talk to, and everyone in my family is blind to anything that's not connected to the wedding."

DeeDee popped a grape into her mouth. "And you still haven't talked to Jana about Jim?"

Patty shook her head. "It's crazy, huh? She's been home almost a week, and we haven't had one private talk yet! Jana's back in her old bedroom, right down the hall from mine, and I miss her as much as if she were still in San Francisco."

"What a drag!" DeeDee exclaimed. "Patty, you have to do something."

"I know," Patty conceded. "But I'm kind of—make that very—mad at her. She doesn't think about anyone but herself these days. I could walk around the house with a paper bag over my head, and she wouldn't notice."

"She's still your sister," DeeDee reminded Patty. "And right after the wedding, she and this Ted person are moving to Germany. If you don't talk to Jana now, who knows when you two will be together again."

Patty knew DeeDee was right. If she didn't talk to Jana soon, she might not get the chance for a long time.

DeeDee went on. "Just go for it, Patty. Steal some time alone with Jana, whatever it takes. Once she hears about what happened with Jim, she'll forget about the wedding for a change and help you with your problem."

"Jana always was a good big sister in the old days," Patty mused. "Maybe I'm not being fair to her. Of course she'll care, once she hears what's been going on with me. I'll tell her today, right after school," Patty vowed.

Patty didn't have dance class on Wednesdays: That was usually the day she stayed after school to meet with the drama club. This afternoon, though, she decided to take the bus straight home after her last class. She was determined to talk to Jana, and she knew that if she waited until later she would never get the chance. Her parents would be home, and they would all sit down to dinner—and start planning the seating arrangements for the rehearsal dinner, or some such thing.

It'll be fun, Patty anticipated, gazing out the bus window at the azure Southern California sky. *We'll make chocolate chip cookies and eat half the batter, like we used to do in the old days when Jana was home on vacation from college. And we'll talk.* It would be such a relief to open up about Jim. Maybe it was too late for advice, but Patty at least needed to know her sister cared what happened to her.

Patty walked quickly down the street from the bus stop. Her parents were carpooling to work these days so that Jana would have the use of a car, and Patty was glad to see it in the driveway. That meant Jana was home, not out on a wedding errand.

She found her sister in the kitchen waiting for the teakettle to whistle. Patty's face lit up with genuine pleasure. She almost felt as though she were seeing Jana for the first time, as if all the chaos and tension of the past five days had never existed. "Jana, hi! I'm glad I caught you alone."

"Why, what's up?" Jana asked briskly.

"Well, I just wanted to talk to you," Patty explained, hastening to steer the conversation in the direction she wanted it to go. "Something's been on my mind. You see, I have this problem, with—"

"Problem!" Jana yelled, just as the teakettle started to shriek. "Not another one!"

Patty stared at her sister, swallowing her own words in surprise.

"There just can't *be* any more problems!" Jana ranted, removing the kettle from the heat and slamming it down again with a bang. She ran a hand through her tousled black curls. "I called the caterers today, thinking all they needed to know about was the menu, and they told me they have to know how many people to serve by the day after tomorrow! And then the florists called. They can't get the gerber daisies I wanted for centerpieces at the reception." Jana ticked the catastrophes off on her fingers one by one. "And would it have occurred to *you*, Patty, that you'd have to hire an organist to play during the ceremony? It sure didn't occur to *me*. I thought it came with the church!" She threw up her hands. "So don't hit me with another problem!"

In an instant, all of Patty's warmth disappeared, and a cold wave of anger and disappointment washed over her. The confused, tumultuous feelings that had been pent up inside her for the past five days burst out, like a cork from a champagne bottle. "I don't want to hear about the florists and the caterers and the dumb organist!" Patty shouted. "I'm sick and tired of hearing about this wedding! Don't you think anyone's entitled to have a problem besides you?"

Now it was Jana's turn to be struck speechless. Patty went on, driven by the force of her emotions. "The wedding's all you care about," she accused Jana, hot tears of resentment filling her eyes. "I might as well not exist anymore! I don't feel close to you—I don't even feel like we're sisters. Maybe you'd better get somebody else to be your maid of honor, Jana, because I don't want to have anything to do with your wedding. I never want to hear the word 'wedding' again!"

Patty stopped, flushed and breathless. Jana was frozen in place, a tea bag in one hand. A variety of emotions crossed her face—first shock and disbelief, then hurt and fury.

"Fine," Jana snapped back, her dark eyes flashing. "It's been obvious from the start that you weren't the least bit interested in Ted and me and our engagement. You've been sulking like a five-year-old for days. I'll be *glad* to find someone to take your place!" Throwing the tea bag onto the counter, Jana stormed past Patty on her way out of the kitchen. "I don't want you in my wedding after all!"

Ten

"Patty, I brought you some fresh-squeezed orange juice. Can I come in?"

It was Sunday morning. Patty had been up for an hour or more, and she was already dressed, sitting cross-legged on her neatly made bed, flipping through a dance magazine.

At the sound of Mrs. Gilbert's voice, Patty tensed. She knew why her mother was offering room service this morning. Patty and Jana's fight had blossomed into a full-fledged feud—they hadn't voluntarily spoken to each other since Wednesday. Jana wouldn't even remain in the same room as Patty, and Patty had managed to miss dinner four nights running. To top things off, Patty had tried a few more times to reach Jim at college. After her last attempt on Friday, she had given up. He was never around, and she figured there was no use torturing herself about it anymore.

Mom's going to try to patch things up between Jana and me, Patty guessed, closing the magazine. *She knows I can't come up with a good excuse for turning down fresh-squeezed orange juice.* "Sure, Mom," she called, resigning herself to the conversation. "Come on in."

Mrs. Gilbert entered, carrying a tray with a glass of juice, a blueberry muffin, and a small vase of fresh-cut flowers from the garden in the backyard.

Patty smiled in spite of herself. "Mom, you didn't have to go to all this trouble. I was going to grab some breakfast in a few minutes."

Mrs. Gilbert rested the tray on the night table. "Were you just waiting to make sure Jana had cleared out of the kitchen before you put in an appearance?" she asked, her soft voice tinged with reproach.

Patty's smile faded. She reached for the juice, not meeting her mother's gaze. "I was just doing some reading," Patty said unconvincingly.

Mrs. Gilbert sat on the edge of her daughter's bed. Lifting her hand, she gently pushed the hair back from Patty's forehead. "People asked after you at the bridal shower yesterday," she said. "Of course everyone wondered why you weren't there. I said you had a dance recital you couldn't get out of."

"Thanks," Patty mumbled.

"But a story like that isn't going to wash

next Saturday, at the wedding," Mrs. Gilbert continued.

"I'm sorry, Mom." Patty drew her knees up, hugging them close to her chest. "I don't expect you to cover up for me," she said. "But I'm not changing my mind. I'm not going to the wedding."

Mrs. Gilbert heaved a distressed sigh. "I never thought I'd see the day when you two would let an argument come between you, and at a time like this!"

"I'm sorry, Mom," Patty repeated. "I know this is the hardest on you. But it's not all my fault. Jana's as much to blame as I am." *More to blame!* she added silently to herself.

"I know, honey," her mother said. "But that's not what matters at this point. What matters is that you and your sister make up with each other so that you can be with her on her wedding day. Otherwise, you'll both regret it for the rest of your lives."

"Jana doesn't want me to be in her wedding," Patty reminded her mother coldly.

"I don't think that's true. Jana will bend, if you do," Mrs. Gilbert insisted. "Do the big thing, Patty, and apologize to her. She'll soften up. I'm positive she wants you to be her maid of honor."

"Why should *I* apologize?" Patty demanded stubbornly. "She hurt me first."

Mrs. Gilbert took one of Patty's hands and squeezed it. "Somebody has to take the first step," she urged. "You can do it, Patty, I know you can. It would be a gift to your sister, the best wedding gift she could ever receive. And I know you two love each other, no matter what you may have done or said to the contrary."

When Patty remained silent, Mrs. Gilbert sat back and looked at her, her expression serious. "This is your last chance, honey," she told her daughter. "Jana's going to call Tracy this morning to ask her to be her maid of honor in your place."

Patty had already figured Jana might ask Tracy, their cousin and a junior at Sweet Valley High. Now, for the first time, Patty came face to face with the fact: She wouldn't be in—or at—her own sister's wedding.

The realization created an ache in her heart. *If she really cared, she'd be up here herself asking me to forgive her, instead of planning to find someone to replace me*, Patty told herself.

"No, Mom," Patty said. She hated to disappoint her mother, but she didn't feel she could forgive Jana first. "Jana might as well go ahead and ask Tracy," she said glumly. Rolling over, Patty buried her face in a pillow so that she wouldn't be able to see if her mother started to cry. "I won't be at the wedding, and that's final."

                                *   *   *

"Jessica, what on earth . . .?"

After breakfast, Elizabeth had barged into Jessica's room in search of her sunglasses, which Jessica borrowed on a regular basis. Jessica, her silky hair pulled into a high ponytail and tied with a bandanna, was dressed in her most beat-up jeans and an old tattered shirt of their father's.

Elizabeth burst out laughing. "What, is it Halloween already? Are you going trick-or-treating?"

Jessica had jumped guiltily when Elizabeth entered. She didn't want her T-shirt painting project to be discovered, and up until now she had managed to remain undetected. Now she was caught—her desk was littered with tubes of paint and paintbrushes. Jessica placed her hands on her hips. "No, I'm *not* going trick-or-treating," she retorted. "This is just . . . loungewear."

"Loungewear?" Elizabeth giggled as she picked her way through the clothes on the floor to retrieve the sunglasses from Jessica's cluttered bureau. "Then, what's with the art supplies? You're not going to paint your room again, are you?" she asked in mock horror.

Jessica grinned. A few years ago, deciding she needed a change of scene, she had painted her bedroom walls a dark chocolate brown. Since then her family had disparagingly referred to her room as "The Hershey Bar." "Don't give me any ideas!" she kidded Elizabeth, looking for a way to change the subject. "Where are you off to, anyway?"

"Secca Lake for a hike and picnic with Todd, Enid, and Hugh," Elizabeth answered. "But, Jessica, what's all that paint for? What are you doing?"

"Oh, I'm just messing around. I was inspired at the crafts fair last weekend," Jessica explained lamely. "A hike at Secca Lake, huh? That sounds like fun," she hastened to add, even though it sounded boring to her. "Well, you must be in a hurry. See you later!"

Elizabeth didn't take the hint. Instead, she crossed the room to get a closer look at the white undershirt spread out on Jessica's desk. "Hey, you're painting a T-shirt, just like DeeDee!"

"Well, yeah, sort of," Jessica admitted. She didn't have to tell Liz she was painting half a dozen T-shirts. "I thought it looked like fun. You know me, I'll try anything for fashion."

Elizabeth shook her head. "Yeah, I know you. But I'd have figured you'd *buy* a painted T-shirt before you'd *make* one any day!"

Jessica shrugged her shoulders and gave her twin an impish smile. "What can I say? I'm full of surprises."

"That's for sure." Elizabeth laughed. "No one ever said Jessica Wakefield was the least bit predictable." She turned to head out. "Well, have a fun day, Jess."

105

Jessica nodded, her earrings swinging. "I will. You, too."

The glittering earrings caught Elizabeth's eye. "Jess, those earrings are really pretty. Are they new?"

Jessica put a hand to her ears. "These? Yeah, I bought them last weekend at the crafts fair."

The earrings were made of silver beads strung with tiny shells. Elizabeth moved closer to admire them. "I guess there's no chance you bought an extra pair for me?" she asked.

Jessica laughed. "Sorry. As usual, cash was limited. But you can borrow them any time. In fact, if you want to wear them today, you can," she volunteered. Jessica was ready to give the earrings to Elizabeth outright—anything to get rid of her, so she could get back to painting. She had only finished one T-shirt so far, and Vincent was expecting at least two more by Tuesday.

"That's all right," Elizabeth said. "I'll just have to visit the next crafts fair."

"You know who could get you a pair if you really like them? Patty Gilbert," Jessica suggested.

"Patty?" Elizabeth inquired.

"Yeah. Her boyfriend's cousin made them," she informed Elizabeth. "Jim Hollis's cousin. I forget her name, but I think she came up from L.A. for the weekend."

"Jim Hollis's cousin?" Elizabeth repeated.

Jessica didn't have all day to stand around talking if she wanted to paint a T-shirt or two and still have time to tan for a while by the pool. She practically shoved Elizabeth out the door. "Bye, Liz. Have fun on your nature trail!"

Elizabeth stood in the hall outside Jessica's bedroom, her mind working rapidly. She thought back to Patty's story about seeing Jim with another girl at the movies the previous weekend. That girl must have been Jim's cousin from L.A., the girl Jessica bought the earrings from at the crafts fair! *Chances are Jim isn't seeing another girl after all*, Elizabeth deduced. *Patty has to hear about this!*

She looked at her watch. She was meeting Todd, Enid, and Hugh at Enid's house at eleven-thirty. That gave her just enough time to swing by Patty's on the way.

A few minutes later Elizabeth was on her way. After parking at the curb in front of the Gilberts' house, she hurried to the front door and rang the bell. A slender girl with curly black hair answered. Elizabeth guessed it was Patty's sister, the one who was getting married.

"Hi, I'm Liz Wakefield, a friend of Patty's," she said with a friendly smile. "Is she home?"

Jana had opened the door with a polite smile on her face. Now she narrowed her eyes.

"Sorry," she said, the coolness of her voice surprising Elizabeth. "Patty's out grocery shopping with my mother."

Elizabeth frowned. "I really need to talk to her," she said. "I have some important news about Jim."

"Jim?" Jana's expression softened somewhat. "Has something happened to him?" she asked, concerned. "I've been wondering—I've been home for a week, and he hasn't called Patty once. Usually they gab on the phone all the time."

Elizabeth's eyes widened. "Didn't Patty tell you? They broke up last weekend!"

Jana gasped, clearly astonished. *Why wouldn't Patty tell her own sister about something like this?* Elizabeth wondered, puzzled. At that moment a car pulled up the driveway and into the open garage. "There's Patty now," Jana said. "Come on in."

Elizabeth followed Jana down the hall to the big country-style kitchen. Patty and Mrs. Gilbert were just entering from the side door, their arms filled with brown grocery bags.

"Thanks," Elizabeth said, turning to Jana.

Jana shrugged. "No problem." The angry, tight look had returned to her face as soon as Patty entered the room.

"Hi, Liz! What are you doing here?" Patty called in greeting, ignoring her sister.

Without a word, Jana turned sharply on her heel and marched out of the kitchen.

Elizabeth could practically hear the tension crackling. Patty and Jana weren't talking to each other; they weren't even looking at each other. *What is going on?* she wondered.

Patty dumped the two grocery bags she was carrying on top of the counter. "Have you been here long?" she asked Elizabeth, feeling a little anxious. She could imagine the reception any friend of hers would have gotten from Jana.

"Only a minute," Elizabeth said. "And I can't stay. But I really wanted to talk to you about something."

"Sure. Let's go upstairs." Patty glanced at her mother. "OK if I leave you with all these bags, Mom?"

Mrs. Gilbert nodded. "Go ahead, you two. I'll put this stuff away."

In a moment Patty had whisked Elizabeth up to her bedroom. Elizabeth took the desk chair, and Patty sat on the edge of her bed. "What's up?" Patty asked. She couldn't begin to guess why Elizabeth would look so serious. "Is there a problem with that 'Personal Profiles' article?"

Elizabeth shook her head. "It's something I heard from Jessica just now, something about Jim."

"Jim!" Patty exclaimed. "What?"

"Last weekend when Jim was home and you saw him at the movies with another girl—well, the same weekend, Jim's cousin from L.A. was in town visiting his family. Jessica met her at the crafts fair. She had a booth there."

"Jim's *cousin*?" Patty repeated blankly. "A booth at the crafts fair?" For a second she didn't get it. Then all of a sudden Patty felt as if the floor had dropped out from under her. Everything made sense—too much sense. "You mean the girl I saw Jim with at the movies was probably his cousin?" Patty asked, dismayed and happy at the same time.

Elizabeth nodded. "It looks like it."

"I can't believe I could be so stupid as to jump to conclusions like that!" Patty moaned, putting her face in her hands. "I'm so embarrassed."

"Anybody could have made the same mistake," Elizabeth pointed out gently.

"After the movie when we had the fight on the phone," Patty remembered, a sick feeling in her stomach, "Jim was probably calling to explain about his cousin. I didn't give him a chance."

"Now that you know what was going on, maybe you can patch things up with him," Elizabeth suggested.

A spark of hope flickered inside Patty for the first time in days. "Maybe," she said weakly.

Elizabeth stood up. "I've got to run. But give me a call later if you want to talk some more."

Patty walked Elizabeth out to the curb. "Thanks, Liz!" she called, waving as the Fiat pulled away. Then she turned back toward the house, her mind in a whirl. She had made a mistake last weekend at the movies, a serious mistake. She prayed that Jim would forgive her for accusing him unjustly.

Patty ran into the house and took the stairs to the second floor two at a time. In her bedroom, she riffled through her desk for some paper and a pen. She sat down and smoothed her hand over the top sheet. Then she started writing. Her pen flew across the page, impelled by the force of her feelings.

Dear Jim,
I'm probably the last person you want to hear from after the things I said the last time we talked. But I didn't mean any of it. It was all an awful mix-up! I found out today that the girl at the movies was your cousin. I know I should have trusted you and I should have given you a chance to explain. I regret it now so much, because I miss you like crazy. I never wanted to argue with you in the first place. I just wanted to spend some time with my sister, and even that's turned into a disaster! Jana's

getting married, and I was supposed to be her maid of honor, but then she and I had a big fight, and now we're not speaking to each other. It seems like everything in my life has gone wrong lately. I'm confused about so many things, but there's one thing I'm sure of: I care about you more than anyone in the world. Do you still love me? Can we try again?

Patty paused, her hand cramped from scribbling so rapidly. She stared down at the page, rereading her words. They had come straight from her heart: she had never meant anything more in her life.

But as she read the letter a second time, she started to feel less certain. Jim probably didn't want to receive a letter from her. He obviously didn't want to talk to her again, or he would have tried to contact her at least once. Perhaps he wasn't involved with another girl, but it was still clear he didn't want to have anything to do with Patty anymore.

Pushing the sheet of paper away from her, Patty dropped her head on her arms and let her tears fall. She might as well face facts once and for all. Jim was out of her life, forever.

Eleven

"A taxi won't do me any good an hour from now, but thanks, anyway," Jana said in a clipped tone on Monday afternoon. She slammed down the phone in frustration.

She had tried all the cab companies listed in the yellow pages, but none of them had a taxi free to pick her up for at least a half hour. *It looks as if I'm really stranded*, Jana thought. Her dress fitting at the bridal shop was at four o'clock, in just fifteen minutes. So much was going on that she had gotten two appointments confused and thought her fitting was at five-thirty.

Once more, Jana glanced anxiously at the clock on the kitchen wall. Her parents had carpooled again. They had allowed Patty to take the car that day because she had had to go to the dentist after school, and without the car, she wouldn't make it to her dance class. Mrs. Gilbert, thinking Jana's appointment was at five-thirty, had told Jana that Patty would be back in time with the car. Not for the first time, Jana wished she hadn't already sold her VW.

Just then, the flash of sunlight on metal caught Jana's eye. Her spirits lifted as she looked out the window. There was the Buick in the driveway. Patty was home early! Maybe she didn't need the car. No, she thought. Patty would never miss a dance class. She must have come home to get something.

Jana drummed her fingers on the kitchen counter, considering the situation. She would have to ask Patty for a ride—and they hadn't even spoken in five days! But she didn't have a choice at this point. The fitting would be impossible to reschedule at this late date.

Two days earlier, Jana would have preferred walking the five miles downtown to asking Patty for a ride. Patty's indifference over her engagement had hurt Jana deeply, and Jana was still smarting from her sister's violent outburst the previous week. The two had had plenty of spats over the years, but never a disagreement of this magnitude.

However, Jana had done a lot of thinking since she had learned about Patty's breakup with Jim. As mad as she was at her sister, Jana couldn't help feeling bad for her, knowing how much she must be hurting inside over Jim. *Well,*

114

I guess I'll swallow my pride, she decided. *I have to!*

A moment later Patty rushed into the kitchen from the side door. She looked surprised when Jana didn't make tracks as soon as she appeared. Instead of leaving in a huff, Jana blocked Patty's path.

"Patty, I need a huge favor from you," Jana said. "I wouldn't ask you if I didn't have to. Do you need the car?"

"Yes, I need the car," Patty said coldly. "I forgot my tights and just came home for them."

Jana took a deep breath, and asked, "Then could you please drive me to Elaine's Bridals downtown on your way to dance class? I'm about to miss my fitting."

Patty's eyes narrowed. "Sorry, but I'm running late as it is. I really don't have time—"

"Please, Patty?" Jana begged. "I really can't miss this appointment. It won't take long. You'll still make it to class. Please?"

Patty couldn't ignore the desperate look on Jana's face. "All right, I'll drive you," she relented. "Just let me run upstairs for a second."

The sisters didn't speak a word on the way to town. Jana stared out the car window while Patty drove rapidly to the dress shop, annoyed that she was going to be late for dance and also annoyed that she had been cornered into doing something nice for Jana. This was the closest the two had been to each other since their big fight, and Patty felt uncomfortable about it. It was easier to turn a cold shoulder to somebody when you could make your point by leaving the room. Now, all of a sudden, it seemed unnatural, even silly, that she and Jana weren't speaking to each other.

But Patty wasn't about to give up being mad at Jana. *It's the same story all over again,* she thought, turning onto Sweet Valley's Main Street. *Jana's just thinking about herself. She wouldn't bother to talk to me if she didn't need me for something.*

Patty pulled into a parking space in front of the bridal shop. "Here we are. I'll pick you up after my class," she said in a peeved tone.

Jana stared at her. "You mean you're not coming in with me?"

"I have to get to class," Patty announced stiffly.

"Oh, please come in, Pat," Jana pleaded. "Since Mom's not here, I need your opinion about the dress and veil."

"Ms. Boydston hates it when people are late," Patty said, unbuckling her seat belt. "So you'd better hurry."

Inside Elaine's, two seamstresses were waiting. As soon as Jana appeared, they whisked her into a curtained-off dressing area. Patty wandered around the shop browsing through the racks of formal gowns and then took a seat on a folding chair, fidgeting as more and more minutes passed. *At this rate I might as well forget about dance class,* she thought, checking her watch. *Why did I bother to bring Jana here, anyway? And why did I agree to come in? For all I care, she can get married in a burlap sack!*

Patty looked up from the bridal magazine she had been flipping through just as Jana emerged from the changing room in her wedding dress. Patty gasped.

Jana turned slowly around so her sister could see the dress from all sides. "What do you think, Patty?" she asked, her expression shy and hopeful.

"Oh, Jana," Patty breathed. "It's absolutely beautiful. You look just like a picture from this magazine!"

The ivory dress made Jana's brown skin glow. Tiny bead-embroidered flowers decorated the bodice while the full-length skirt fell in soft, flowing tiers. As Jana twirled around, her sheer, lace-edged veil fluttered with the movement.

All of a sudden, Patty's eyes filled with tears. The sight of Jana in her wedding dress brought back so many fond memories. Jana posing in her first prom dress while Patty gazed on admiringly . . . Jana looking distinguished in her cap and gown on the day she graduated from college. . . . Everything Jana had meant to her over the years came rushing back, and Patty felt her anger dissolving. *Why on earth are we in this ridiculous feud?* she wondered.

Without thinking, Patty hopped up from her chair and darted across the shop. She hugged Jana close, being careful not to crush the delicate fabric.

Laughing, Jana wiped the tears off Patty's cheeks, not seeming to notice there were a few on her own. "I'm glad you approve. I hope Ted likes it as much!"

Fifteen minutes later, Jana was back in her street clothes. She set a time to pick up the dress on Friday and then followed Patty out to the parking lot. Inside the car, the sisters looked at each other for a long moment. Jana fiddled nervously with the strap of her pocketbook, while Patty clutched the steering wheel tightly.

"Jana, I—" she began.

"You know, Pat—"

Patty laughed. "Go ahead, you first."

"OK." Jana grinned. "I just wanted to say thanks for driving me. You totally saved the day. But I made you really late for dance, didn't I?"

"Yep," said Patty. "I might as well skip it altogether. That's all right," she added quickly, seeing Jana's crestfallen expression. "I'd rather have done this. Really."

"Thanks," Jana said softly.

Turning the key in the ignition, Patty started the car, then pulled into the traffic on Main Street. As Jana rolled down her window, she chuckled.

"What's so funny?" Patty asked, raising an eyebrow.

"Us! Do you know what just happened?"

"No, what?"

"We actually talked to each other!" Jana's eyes crinkled with wry amusement. "Does that mean the feud's off?"

Patty wasn't feeling especially angry with Jana at the moment, but she didn't think she should let her sister win her over so easily. "I'm not sure," she said cautiously.

Jana put a hand on Patty's shoulder, her expression serious. "I know," she said. "I owe you an apology first. You had every right to blow up at me the other day. I've been rotten the whole time I've been home."

"Um-hmm," Patty agreed.

"If anything, I should have been trying to get closer to you instead of driving you away," Jana continued. "After all, a wedding is just one day. Being sisters—that's forever."

Patty glanced at Jana. "That's just what I was thinking back at the bridal shop," she confessed. "I'm sorry, too, Jana. I know I've been touchy lately. And selfish in my own way."

119

"Does this mean you'll be my maid of honor after all?" Jana asked hopefully.

A broad smile brightened Patty's face. "I'd love to. I wouldn't miss out on your big day for anything. What about Tracy, though? Won't she be upset if she can't be in the wedding?"

Jana shook her head. "I doubt it. If anything, I bet she'll be happy to hear we finally made up. She was uncomfortable with the idea of filling in for you."

For the rest of the drive home, Patty and Jana chattered a mile a minute, trying to make up for a week of missed opportunities. "Now, what's this I hear about Jim?" Jana asked as they reached the house and got out of the car.

Patty raised her eyebrows. "What did you hear?"

"That you broke up. Your friend Liz mentioned it, assuming I knew. Do you want to tell me about it?"

"Do I ever!" Patty admitted. "Let's go upstairs."

The conversation adjourned to Patty's bedroom. It only took a few moments to tell Jana the whole story right up to Elizabeth's suspicion that the girl Patty had seen with Jim had been his cousin. "And then I wrote this," Patty said, handing Jana the unmailed letter.

Jana scanned the page. "This is nice. It's sweet and apologetic. So, what are you waiting for? Why haven't you sent it?"

"I was going to." Patty took the letter back from Jana and folded it into a neat square. "But if Jim wanted us to get back together, wouldn't he call? Or at least answer the phone when I called?" Patty shook her head glumly. "His feelings must have changed. I guess I pushed him too far."

"Not to be a bossy big sister, but I'm sure you're wrong," Jana said. "When Jim reads that letter, Patty, he'll understand why you acted the way you did. Anyway, you'll never know how he feels until you let him know how *you* feel."

Patty frowned. "I don't know . . ."

"Look at us," Jana insisted. "If we hadn't started talking, we'd still be fighting with each other for no good reason. Send the letter, Patty."

"I'll think about it," Patty promised. But although she was thrilled to be reconciled with Jana, she wasn't sure Jim would be as eager to make up with her.

Twelve

"Just tell Robin I won't be able to make cheer-leading today," Jessica instructed Amy Sutton. "She can run practice by herself for once."

The two had met at Jessica's locker when the final bell rang, signaling the end of school. Amy watched as Jessica took a plastic garment bag from her locker, then slammed the metal door shut. "What's up that you can't go to practice?" she asked, curious.

"Just tell Robin I can't make it," Jessica repeated, peeved at her friend's nosiness.

It was tempting to tell Amy the whole story about Vincent and the Blue Parrot. Jessica hated keeping secrets, and for the past week she had been dying to announce her latest caper. But she had decided she would rather wait and introduce Vincent to her friends as her new boyfriend at the next boring Sweet Valley High party. That would really shock everybody! In the meantime, she figured it was smart to keep quiet about the circumstances under which she had discovered her latest love interest. She didn't want the T-shirt story getting back to DeeDee even if it did turn out, as Jessica suspected, that Vincent's interest in the shirts was merely a ploy to see her again.

"You'll find out in due time," Jessica promised Amy teasingly. "Now run along to practice."

"Then I'll tell your co-captain you've just decided you can't make practice, for no reason at all," Amy retaliated. "We won't miss you, Jess!"

Laughing, Jessica waved goodbye to Amy and then hurried through the throng of departing students, the garment bag slung over one arm. She ducked into the nearest girls' room. Five minutes later she reemerged into the now empty hallway. Instead of the bright blue tank top and stone-washed miniskirt she had worn to school, Jessica had changed into a boxy, wheat-colored linen jacket and matching knee-length skirt that she had smuggled out of Elizabeth's closet that morning. The jacket sleeves could be rolled up slightly, and with a lacy camisole, her new earrings, and her hair loose, Jessica thought she looked artsy, sophisticated . . . and entirely irresistible.

I'm probably going to need all the help I can get, Jessica admitted to herself as she climbed into the Fiat, parked in the far corner of the Sweet Valley High student lot. She reached behind the driver's seat to retrieve a cardboard clothing box. Lifting the lid, she pulled out the first of five folded T-shirts.

The painted design was certainly bright enough, Jessica observed with some satisfaction. Even so, she had a sinking feeling that, as hard as she had tried to imitate what she remembered of DeeDee's designs, her T-shirts didn't come close. On this particular one, Jessica had attempted an ocean scene in blue and green. Unfortunately, her whale had ended up resembling a big black oil slick, and the palm trees on the mud-colored beach looked like something from a horror movie—green killer spiders from Mars, she thought.

Jessica shoved the T-shirt back into the box and quickly covered it with the lid. *It doesn't matter*, she reminded herself confidently as she cruised toward town, the car radio blasting. *As soon as Vincent sees me, T-shirts will be the farthest thing from his mind!*

She parked the Fiat in front of the Blue Parrot Shop. *Here goes nothing*, she thought as she pushed open the door and stepped inside. The shop was both cluttered and elegant, and Jessica could see at a glance that the merchandise was high quality. She almost burst out laughing, picturing her pathetic T-shirts on display.

124

"Jessica, you're right on time!"

Jessica's heart skipped a few beats at the sound of Vincent's deep, sexy voice. He was walking toward her, one hand held out. "Hi, Vincent," she said, giving him her most dazzling smile as she shifted the cardboard box to her left hand so she could shake with her right.

"Come along to the office," he invited her, placing a hand on her back. Jessica tingled at his touch. "Cassie's waiting for us there."

"Cassie?" In all her daydreaming about Vincent, Jessica had forgotten about his partner. "You know, we don't need to bother her," Jessica suggested. "In fact, if you're busy I could show you the shirts some other time." She lowered her eyelashes provocatively. "We could just talk for a while."

"No, no, no." Vincent continued to usher Jessica in the direction of the office. "I wouldn't ask you to come all this way for nothing. There's no need to be nervous, Jessica. Cassie is going to love your work, I promise you."

Jessica bit her lip. *Want to bet?* she felt like asking.

A tall, slender woman in an emerald silk dress rose to greet Jessica as she entered the office at the back of the store. "Jessica, I've been looking forward to meeting you," Cassie said, her manner friendly but professional. "I'm eager to see the shirts Vincent's told me so much about!" She sat down again, her expression expectant.

Jessica gulped, her mouth suddenly as dry as dust. It didn't appear as though she could expect any help from Vincent: he was waiting for her presentation, too. *I could turn around and sprint out of the store*, she thought desperately. *And never show my face in this part of Sweet Valley again!*

But Jessica wasn't the type to give up without a fight, especially where a gorgeous guy was concerned. Taking a deep breath, she held her shoulders straight and smiled with false confidence. "Let me show you what I brought," she said brightly. She took a deep breath as she opened the cardboard box and pulled out the first T-shirt for Vincent and Cassie to view. In the fluorescent light of the office, the paint job looked even worse than it had in the parking lot.

"I call this one 'Seascape,' " Jessica said, handing it to Vincent and trying to ignore his shocked expression. "And this one—" As Jessica picked up the next T-shirt, she cringed. If anything, her attempt at a mountain range at sunset was even worse than her ocean. "This is called, uh, 'Sierra Sunset.' "

Cassie appeared distinctly puzzled. "*These* are the T-shirts you've been raving about?" she asked, turning to Vincent.

Vincent shook his head, staring at Jessica as if she had suddenly turned into a toad. "These are

126

not the same T-shirts I saw at the crafts fair," he declared, irked. He looked at Jessica for an explanation. "Jessica?"

Think fast, Wakefield! Jessica coached herself. "Uh, I-I tried a new technique with this batch," she sputtered, praying Vincent would buy her story.

Vincent shook his head in disbelief. "If I hadn't seen you with my own eyes, I'd swear you couldn't be the same artist I met at the crafts fair!" he boomed.

Jessica decided it was time to shift from defense to offense. "How dare you imply that I'm some kind of fake!" she cried, putting her hands on her hips. "Obviously you just don't *understand* artistic temperament."

"Artistic temperament?" Vincent repeated.

"Yes, artistic temperament," Jessica repeated. "We artists are always, um, evolving in new directions." She was really getting into her speech now. "Where do you think civilization would be if famous artists didn't experiment?"

"Hear, hear!" cheered Cassie, clearly entertained by this performance.

Jessica was encouraged. "So if you don't appreciate my work," she said with dignity, "I'd just as soon take it somewhere else." She picked up the box and prepared to march out of the room.

"Wait a minute," Vincent said, blocking her

escape route. "An experiment is one thing, but these are"—he paused, searching for the right word—"not *art*," he concluded.

"I've never been so insulted!" Jessica huffed.

"I'm sure the last thing Vincent meant to do was insult you, Jessica," Cassie said soothingly. "You know, I think I like your new experimental technique. Why don't you tell us more about it? Whom do you study art with? What materials do you use, and why?"

What was left of Jessica's hot air emerged in a defeated sigh. Cassie had called her bluff. It was time for true confessions.

"I can't tell a lie," Jessica said. *I sound like George Washington after he chopped down the cherry tree!* "When I met Vincent, I was just helping a friend by watching her booth for a while. *She* painted the T-shirts he saw at the fair—I didn't!"

Vincent's dark eyebrows shot up. "Why on earth did you let me believe that you were the artist?"

"Why?" Jessica stalled. She wasn't about to admit it was because she thought Vincent was attracted to her! It was obvious now that he thought she was as ridiculous as her T-shirts. "I just thought it would be fun to have something I made sold in a store," she said lamely. "I thought I could paint T-shirts as well as anybody."

Cassie laughed. "We're sorry to disillusion you, dear."

"No, I'm sorry for wasting your time," Jessica said. She edged toward the door. "I'll leave now."

128

"Not so fast, Miss Wakefield!" Vincent ordered. "Before you go, I'd like the name of the *real* artist whom you tried to defraud."

"Um, her name is DeeDee Gordon," Jessica mumbled.

"I think I'll call her right now," Vincent announced flipping through the phone book. "Who's name is the listing under?"

Jessica winced as she gave Vincent the name of DeeDee's mother.

"Don't leave quite yet," he added ominously.

Jessica sank weakly onto the nearest chair. The most embarrassing experience of her life wasn't over yet. Vincent was going to tell DeeDee, and DeeDee, who had never liked Jessica much, would probably tell the whole school what she had done. *I'll be the laughingstock of Sweet Valley High!* she realized, resting her face in her hands. *Thanks a lot, Vince, baby!*

"I'm glad Patty and her sister were able to reconcile their differences," Mrs. Gordon remarked.

DeeDee nodded. "Me, too. And I'm invited to the wedding on Saturday. I can't wait!"

DeeDee and her mother were sitting in the family room. When the phone on the desk rang, DeeDee picked it up right away.

"May I speak to DeeDee Gordon?" an unfamiliar male voice requested.

"This is she," DeeDee replied.

"Hello, DeeDee. My name is Vincent Delano, from the Blue Parrot Shop. I spoke to your partner at the Sweet Valley crafts fair about ordering some of your hand-painted T-shirts to sell in my shop."

DeeDee was mystified. "My partner?" she asked. "I don't have a partner."

"I spoke with a Miss Jessica Wakefield," the man explained.

"Jessica!" DeeDee exclaimed, not sure if this information made things any clearer or not.

"Didn't she mention our conversation?"

DeeDee thought back to the fair. Jessica hadn't said a thing when DeeDee returned to the booth after her break. She hadn't sold any T-shirts, either. "No, she didn't," DeeDee told the man.

"Well, I'm sorry about that," Mr. Delano said casually. "But I did admire your work very much, and if you're interested, I would like to meet with you and discuss the possibility of our working together. I really think we could sell a lot of your shirts here at Blue Parrot."

DeeDee was overwhelmed, but she managed to set up an appointment with Mr. Delano for the following week. Then she hung up the phone in a daze.

Why didn't Jessica tell me about all this? she wondered. DeeDee recalled Jessica pumping her for information about T-shirt painting one day

130

during lunch. Something seemed a little fishy here. DeeDee had a vague suspicion that Jessica had been trying to pull another one of her famous stunts.

But at the moment, she was too thrilled to dwell on Jessica's part in this puzzle. "Mom, a store, a real live store, wants to sell my T-shirts!" she cried, throwing her arms around her mother. "I've got to tell Patty. She's not going to believe this!"

"I'll tell Patty you called," Jana promised. "She should be home soon. By the way, DeeDee, I'm glad you can come to Ted's and my wedding. It'll mean a lot to the whole family, having you there. See you then!"

Jana slowly replaced the receiver. She had been upstairs when the phone rang and had picked up the extension in Patty's room since there wasn't one in her own. Now she sat back in Patty's desk chair, daydreaming for a moment about Saturday. It was coming up so fast! But it couldn't come too soon for Jana. She loved Ted so much, she could hardly wait to start their new life together.

Jana came back to reality with a sigh. *If only Patty were as happy as I am*, she thought. It was such a shame that things hadn't worked out with Jim. He and Patty had always been such a cute couple.

Jana glanced down at her sister's desk as she stood up. Out of the corner of her eye, she spotted a piece of folded white paper that looked suspiciously like the letter Patty had shown her a few days ago. Picking up the paper, Jana unfolded it. Sure enough, it was the letter Patty had written to Jim. She had never mailed it.

A split second later, a crazy plan leapt into Jana's mind. She wasn't sure she should interfere with her sister's life, but she knew how much Patty's relationship with Jim meant to her. If she could help get them back together again, wouldn't she be acting like a real sister?

Once Jana made up her mind about something, she stuck with it. Now she reached for the phone without hesitation. She called information, then dialed the number she had been given.

"Hello, Mrs. Hollis? This is Patty Gilbert's sister, Jana. I was wondering if you could give me Jim's address at college. I wanted to mail something to him."

Jana copied the address as Mrs. Hollis dictated it. Then just as she got to the zip code, Jim's mother stopped short. "I almost forgot," said Mrs. Hollis. "Jim won't be at that address until after the weekend. He's gone to the mountains for a two-week geology course. It's an out-of-the-way spot, but if it's important you could send a letter care of general delivery at the local post office. Here, let me give you the address there."

As Jana noted the information, something dawned on her. *A two-week geology course away from campus—that's it!* "Thanks a lot, Mrs. Hollis. Bye, now," she said, grinning from ear to ear.

All at once, it was perfectly clear to Jana why Jim hadn't been in touch with her sister and why there hadn't been any answer at Jim's dorm room whenever Patty tried to call. He hadn't been anywhere near his phone—or any phone, for that matter! Now Jana was doubly sure it was time for her to step in and play matchmaker.

Using a piece of paper from a pad on Patty's desk, Jana scribbled a quick note to Jim, then tucked it along with the letter into an envelope. *I'll take it down to the mailbox on the corner right now,* Jana decided, feeling good about doing something to further her little sister's happiness. *I only hope Jim gets it in time!*

Thirteen

"I like it," Patty commented, raising her voice slightly to be heard over the clatter of typewriters. "I feel like a celebrity, getting a big headline like that!"

She and Elizabeth were in the newspaper office after school on Thursday going over the typeset copy of the "Personal Profiles" interview.

"There'll be a picture, too," Elizabeth told her.

"Full-page, I hope," Patty kidded.

Elizabeth laughed. "You bet!"

"I think you wrote a great article," Patty said.

"Thanks. I'm sure the new column will be a major hit."

"I'm pretty happy with it myself," Liz admitted. "I can't wait to see it in print in next week's *Oracle*!"

Patty had been perched on the one clean corner of Elizabeth's cluttered desk. Now she stood up. "I have to take off. Ted's parents get into town today, and they're coming over for dinner. My mom needs help cleaning and cooking— and to keep her from panicking."

"That's right," said Liz. "The wedding's in two days!"

Patty nodded. "Jana's getting more and more nervous, believe me. She's meeting the Brewsters for the first time tonight. And then everything gets started tomorrow. There's a rehearsal at the church, and then Ted's folks are hosting a dinner at the Valley Inn."

"That's a great spot," Elizabeth observed, feeling a nostalgic pang. The last time she had been at the beautiful seaside restaurant was with Jeffrey French, shortly before they broke up. "Well, in case I don't see you tomorrow, have a great time."

Patty smiled. "You'll hear about it if I trip walking down the aisle."

"Hey, Liz!"

Elizabeth turned to look over her shoulder. Jessica had just waltzed into the newspaper office. Her hand was extended. "Can I have the car keys? I want to hit the Dairi Burger with Amy. I'll swing by to pick you up later."

"You must be starving after that brutal cheerleading practice," Elizabeth joked, rummaging in her book bag for the keys.

Jessica put her hands on her hips. "It's more work than you might imagine, Liz," she said haughtily. "Hi, Patty."

"Hi," Patty said, turning to face Elizabeth's twin.

Jessica's eyes widened slightly, and her face seemed to pale. She looked like she was going to be sick. "Jess, are you all right?" Elizabeth asked. "Maybe you *do* need to get some food in your stomach."

Jessica was staring at Patty's T-shirt, and Patty looked down at it. "DeeDee painted this," she explained, running her fingers along the hem. "You probably remember it from the crafts fair."

"Um-hmm," Jessica mumbled weakly.

"How did your own painting project go?" Patty asked. "I remember you asking DeeDee for some tips."

Jessica grimaced. "It was more trouble than it was worth. I decided I like my T-shirts plain."

Elizabeth laughed. "Whatever happened to your spectacular creation, anyway?"

"Never mind." Jessica snatched the car keys from Elizabeth's hand and headed for the door. "I really need a milkshake. See you!"

"I'd like to make a toast," Mr. Brewster announced, rising to his feet.

Everyone at the rehearsal dinner at the Valley

Inn turned to look at Ted's father. "Ted is our only son and our only child," Mr. Brewster began. "Martha and I are delighted at the prospect of finally having a daughter, too! We're proud of you, Son, and wish both of you all the happiness in the world, tomorrow and every day after."

"Cheers!" everyone yelled. As the cry echoed around the room, Patty took a sip of her iced tea. Then she brushed at her eyes with her napkin. It seemed to her that each toast was mushier than the last. *Or maybe it's just me*, Patty thought.

The evening had been emotional from the start. Before dinner, there had been a brief wedding rehearsal at the church. It was going to be a simple, casual ceremony with just one bridal attendant, Patty, and a best man, a friend of Ted's from the Air Force, Marshall Borden. But even so, as she walked through the steps at the minister's direction with her sister and Ted, Patty felt overwhelmed with emotions. In the cool solemnity of the church, for the first time in two weeks the wedding seemed *real*.

"What, no appetite?" Jana came up behind Patty's chair and put an arm around her sister. "I'm the one who's supposed to be too nervous to eat, silly."

Patty smiled down at her untouched dessert. "I'd offer it to you, Jana, but if you eat another piece of cheesecake, you won't fit into your wedding dress tomorrow," she kidded.

Jana shook a finger at her sister. "Don't pick a fight with me, Patty," she whispered, teasing. "We don't want to start another war at this point!"

As Jana moved on to chat with some out-of-town relatives at the next table, Patty did her best to keep the smile on her face. It was hard. Of course she was happy for her sister. The mood in the inn was joyous, and everyone had been very nice to her, especially Ted's parents. But despite it all, Patty couldn't help having sad thoughts because she couldn't help thinking about Jim.

Pretending to look out the window at the inn's spectacular view of the moonlit Pacific, Patty dabbed at another tear. The setting was so romantic—that was why she and Jim had chosen to have dinner at the inn a few months ago on their "anniversary," two years from the night of their first date. They had sat at a table by the window, but although the sunset had been a dazzling display of red and orange, they had hardly noticed the view or the four-star food. They had been too wrapped up in each other to care about anything else in the world.

Patty sighed as Marshall stood up to offer a toast to his best friend, Ted. *Jim should be here with me*, she thought wistfully.

Marshall's humorous remarks about his old roommate drew lots of good-natured laughs from the crowd, and Patty turned to see how the groom-to-be was taking it. To her surprise, Ted didn't even seem to be listening. And as soon as Marshall was done speaking, Ted checked his watch and quietly slipped out of the room.

Patty didn't think much of it at first. But twenty minutes later after coffee and dessert, when all the guests began to leave and Ted still hadn't returned, Patty couldn't help wondering where he had gone.

Patty joined her radiant sister, who was receiving good-night hugs from various friends. "Jana, where did Ted take off to so suddenly?" she asked as soon as they were alone. "There's nothing wrong, is there?"

"Ted?" Jana repeated, as casually as if Patty had been asking after the waiter instead of her future husband. "Oh, I don't know, Patty," she said lightly. "He doesn't tell me everything. We're not married yet, you know!"

Patty frowned at her sister's response as she wandered out to the restaurant lobby with the rest of the group. Was she the only person who thought it was strange for the groom to be in such a big hurry to leave the bride's side the night before the wedding? Not for the first time, it occurred to Patty that she barely knew Ted.

She only hoped Jana was more sure of him than she was.

Jana woke Patty up at five-thirty on Saturday morning. "I can't sleep," she confessed, her eyes bright with nervous excitement. Patty smiled sleepily. Her big sister looked just like a little kid on Christmas morning. "I've been lying in bed for half an hour, wishing I had somebody to talk to," Jana went on. "Finally I decided I was entitled to wake you up. After all, it's the last time I'll be able to."

Patty sat up and placed a pillow behind her back. Jana was right. After today, things would never be the same. Jana would live with Ted in Germany, and the sisters would only be together on occasional holidays. "Don't make me cry," Patty begged her sister. "If I start now, I won't stop all day."

"Me, either." Jana smiled. "And I don't want my eyes to be all red and puffy when it's time for me to walk down the aisle at eleven-thirty."

The two sisters were silent for a moment. Then they both spoke at once. "I can't believe you're getting married!" Patty cried.

"I can't believe I'm getting married!" Jana said at the same time. She laughed. "It's just so strange. For the first time in my life, I really feel like I'm grown-up. I mean, this is it."

Patty nodded. Marriage was such a big step. As she took it, Jana would be leaving Patty far behind.

The next few hours passed in a whirl. The florist delivery truck arrived with the flower arrangements for the reception and Jana's and Patty's bouquets but then had to make a second trip, having forgotten the men's boutonnieres. The photographer was taking light readings in the living room while the caterers were trying to set up tables for the luncheon. Neighbors kept dropping by with wedding day wishes and gifts. Meanwhile, Jana and Patty dashed in and out of the upstairs bathroom, taking turns showering and doing their makeup and hair.

At last Patty was dressed. She looked at her reflection in the full-length mirror on the back of her bedroom door. She felt formal in the stiff, polished-cotton dress and brand-new high-heeled shoes. Around her neck was the gold chain and pearl pendant Jana had given her the night before as a thank-you gift for acting as her maid of honor. Patty glanced at her clock radio. It was eleven. In half an hour, they would be at the church! *I'm ready*, she thought, straightening her sash.

Patty practiced a dignified down-the-aisle style of walk as she headed toward her sister's room. Reaching Jana's door, she knocked softly.

"Come in!" Jana called.

141

Patty opened the door slowly. She had already seen Jana in her wedding dress at the bridal shop, but Patty was still overwhelmed by the sight of her sister. Her cheeks and eyes glowing, Jana looked more beautiful than Patty had ever seen her. "Patty, you're just the person I wanted to see," Jana said, smiling at her. "Would you help me with my veil?"

Patty went to Jana's side, being careful not to step on the hem of her gown. They stood together in front of the mirror over Jana's bureau as Patty used bobby pins to secure the beaded headpiece that held the veil. As she inserted the last pin, Patty's eyes filled with tears. She had never felt so close to her sister, and she wondered if she ever would again. *Maybe on my wedding day*, Patty thought sadly. *Whenever that may be . . .*

Jana caught sight of Patty's expression in the mirror. Turning, she gave her younger sister a hug. "Patty, you mean so much to me," Jana whispered. "I'm so lucky to have a sister like you. Promise you'll write to me in Germany?"

Patty nodded. "I promise. I'll even sneak in a phone call now and then, if Mom and Dad let me. I want us to stay close."

"So do I," Jana said fervently. She seemed to sense that there was more than one reason for Patty's tears. "As for Jim," she added, wiping Patty's damp cheeks with a tissue from a box on her bureau, "who knows? Things might work out for you two after all."

Patty forced a smile. She wished there was a chance of that more than Jana or anyone else would ever know! But it didn't matter how hard she hoped for a miracle to bring her and Jim back together; it wasn't going to happen.

I'm not going to think about it, Patty determined, straightening Jana's veil. It was her sister's wedding day, after all. There would be plenty of time to miss Jim tomorrow, and every day after that.

"Dad, I'm so nervous!" Patty whispered as they stood in the back of the church listening to the organist's prelude.

"Me, too," admitted Mr. Gilbert, smoothing the lapels of his morning coat. "I've never been the father of the bride before."

In a minute the processional music would begin, and Patty would have to walk down the long church aisle all by herself. All of a sudden she thought of at least a dozen things that could go wrong. *I'll drop my bouquet. I'll trip. I'll fall flat on my face in the middle of the church.* Patty was already certain she would burst out crying when the ceremony started.

"You look gorgeous," Jana assured Patty, squeezing her sister's hand. "Pat, you're as

cold as ice! Don't tell me you've got the jit-
ters, too."

"I'm shaking," Patty confessed.

"But you've performed in front of an audi-
ence zillions of times before, in your dance re-
citals," Jana reminded her.

Patty shook her head. "This is different, silly!"

At that moment, the organ music swelled
with a triumphant note. It was the processional—time for Patty to get going! She gave
her sister one last kiss on the cheek. Then, her
heart pounding, she took her first tremulous
step down the aisle.

For a split second she hesitated, gripping her
bouquet tightly. Then she took another step
forward. The small group of wedding guests
stood to watch her entrance. Patty glimpsed
DeeDee sitting in the rear of the church. DeeDee
gave her a wink and a little wave of encourage-
ment.

Patty took a deep breath, then continued
slowly and gracefully down the aisle, the way
she had practiced. To keep calm she focused on
Ted, who was standing at the altar, an eager
look on his face as he awaited the appearance of
his bride. Then Patty's racing heart—and her
feet—nearly stopped. There was a tall, handsome young man in a gray suit standing on the
aisle in the second row of pews, and he was
grinning widely at her.

144

I'm dreaming, Patty thought, walking down the aisle in a robotlike daze. *This has to be a dream.*

But when she reached the front row of pews, right before she moved on to take her place at the altar, Jim bent forward to plant a quick kiss on her cheek. For a brief second that felt like an eternity, he squeezed her hand tightly, and the smile that appeared on Patty's face came straight from her heart.

Fourteen

The ceremony passed in a quick, happy blur. Patty looked back and forth from her sister and Ted to Jim, who didn't take his eyes off her the entire time. It seemed like only a minute or two, and then the minister was pronouncing Ted and Jana husband and wife. They kissed, then Patty found herself walking back up the aisle on Marshall's arm.

On the steps of the church, family and friends crowded around to hug and congratulate the newly married couple. For Patty, though, Jana and Ted could wait. The only person she wanted to see was Jim.

Rushing out of the church, Jim reached Patty in one bound. Without a word, he threw his arms around her and lifted her right off the ground. "Jim, what are you doing here?" Patty squealed. "How did you know—but aren't you mad at me? Why didn't you—"

Jim burst out laughing. Before Patty could get a full sentence out, he had put his mouth on hers for a long, warm kiss.

For a wonderful moment, Patty forgot the hows, whats, and whys of the situation. All that mattered was that Jim was here with her, that he still loved her as much as she loved him.

Resting her cheek against Jim's chest, Patty clasped her hands together behind his back and held him close. "I can't believe you're really here," she said softly.

"Me, either," Jim agreed. "What a crazy couple of weeks this has been, huh?"

Patty pulled away so she could look Jim in the eyes. "Why are you here, really?" she asked, still feeling dazzled and off-balance.

"Because of a letter I got in the mail on Thursday," he said. "A letter that turned my life back around."

"A letter?" Patty was confused. "But I didn't mail that letter . . ."

"No, but someone else did," he said, a twinkle in his eye.

"Jana!" Patty guessed.

Jim nodded. "She sent it, saying you'd chickened out of mailing it yourself. She wrote a note of her own telling me to call her at home while you were at school. So I did, and we talked for a long time. She told me everything—how the wedding had put a real strain between the two of you. She didn't have to talk me into wanting to see you again, though." Jim kissed Patty again. They sat down on the stone steps of the church, and Jim put his arm around Patty's waist. "I was already feeling we'd made a big mistake, letting that stupid fight split us up. As soon as I read the letter, I was ready to hit the road and hitchhike home."

"Hitchhike? What about your car?" Patty asked, confused.

"That's just it. I didn't have my car. I was in the mountains for a two-week geology class expedition. We were totally cut off from civilization." He grinned. "No running water, no TV, no phones—nothing!"

"Then how did Jana get in touch with you?"

"My mom told her to mail the letter to general delivery at the local post office," Jim explained. "I called Jana from a pay phone right then and there."

"So that's why you weren't around when I called," Patty said softly.

"I was planning to call you as soon as I got back to Pacific, when we'd both had time to cool off," Jim told her. "Guess I don't need to now!"

He was about to kiss her again, but Patty held him off. "Wait a minute! There's still one thing I don't get. If you were stranded in the mountains, how did you get to Sweet Valley in time for the wedding?"

"That was Ted's idea," Jim answered. "When Jana told him my geology course bus wasn't heading back to school until Sunday night, Ted volunteered to drive up after the rehearsal dinner to get me. He said he was happy to go out of his way to help out his new sister-in-law. What a guy, huh?"

That explains last night, and Ted's early departure from the Valley Inn! Patty thought. "I'll be right back," she told Jim, jumping to her feet.

She wiggled her way through the cluster of people surrounding Ted and Jana and then threw her arms around both of them at once. "Thanks, you guys!" she said, giving them each a kiss.

Jana smiled. "Anytime," Ted said with a grin. Patty squeezed her sister's hand and then hurried back to Jim. She hated to let him out of her sight even for a moment, after coming so close to losing him.

"I'm pretty lucky to have such a great sister and brother-in-law, huh?" Patty said.

Jim kissed her on the tip of the nose. "You bet."

"And a great boyfriend. That is, if you still are," she added uncertainly. "My boyfriend, I mean."

"I am, if you'll have me," Jim said, shy and

149

serious. "After all, I started the whole thing by acting like a baby when you told me our weekend was off because your sister was in town."

"I was just as bad," Patty reminded him. "And I'm the one who didn't give you a chance to explain about your cousin that night after the movie."

Jim shook his head. "That wasn't your fault. How were you supposed to know she was my cousin? And anyway, I wasn't just calling to explain about Monica. I was also calling to demand an explanation from you about the guy *you* were with!"

Then they both laughed. "How can this seem funny now?" Patty asked ruefully.

"Because it all worked out for the best. We got a happy ending, just like the movies."

"Better than the movies," Patty whispered just as Jim's lips met hers.

It was almost time to leave for the reception back at the Gilberts' house. Earlier that morning, Patty had been dreading the party, knowing she would have to force herself to smile for three or four hours straight. Now she knew smiling wasn't going to be a problem at all!

"I'm sorry about what happened," she said, laying her head on Jim's shoulder. "If I've learned anything, it's that I should trust you the way my heart tells me to, and not let my mind trick me into being jealous."

150

"You don't have any reason to be jealous," Jim promised her. "There's no one else in my life. I love you, Patty."

"I love you, too. Let's never argue again," Patty begged earnestly.

"Oh, no, we can argue," Jim corrected her. "But we have to remember to always give each other the benefit of the doubt. No temper tantrums and no hanging up on each other!"

Patty smiled. "It's a deal."

"What do you say we seal it with a kiss?" Jim suggested.

Patty didn't break away from the embrace even when she heard her sister announce that she was ready to throw her bouquet. *I don't need to catch it*, Patty thought happily. *All my dreams have already come true!*

"According to DeeDee, Patty's family kept the whole thing a total surprise," Elizabeth told Jessica, Todd, and the twins' older brother, Steven, who was home from college for the weekend.

It was Sunday afternoon, and the four were lounging on the patio after a quick game of volleyball in the pool. "Patty walked into the church, and there was Jim! They made up right after the wedding." Elizabeth sighed dreamily, reaching over to squeeze Todd's hand. "Isn't that the most romantic thing you've ever heard?"

Jessica pursed her lips, the expression on her face lemon-sour. Sometimes her twin was such a sap! "I don't think it's so romantic," she announced, pushing her sunglasses higher on the bridge of her nose. "And Patty's a wimp to let Jim get her back so easily. Odds are he's not so wonderful. In my opinion, there's not a decent boy—or man—within a thousand miles of Sweet Valley! Sorry, Todd and Steve," she added as an afterthought.

"Why so down on the male population, Jess?" Steven asked, his brown eyes twinkling with good humor.

"Just a general observation," Jessica answered airily, rolling over on her rainbow-striped beach towel.

Inside, though, she was remembering the Vincent Delano disaster. He had turned out to be such a total jerk! How could she ever have thought he was cute? Fortunately, he had let her off the hook about the T-shirts. She had only escaped major humiliation because he hadn't told DeeDee that Jessica had posed as the artist in her place. When DeeDee asked her about it, Jessica was able to convince her that she had merely forgotten to tell her about Vincent's offer.

Jessica was over her disappointment about

Vincent by now. But one thing was more clear to her than ever. Her love life needed revving up, and how!

One way or another, it's time to take radical action, Jessica told herself. *Mr. Right is out there somewhere, and I'm going to find him if it's the last thing I do!*

What kind of scheme does Jessica have planned to meet the boy of her dreams? Find out in Sweet Valley High #62, WHO'S WHO?